Out of t

The Dearne High was designated a Specialist Humanities College in September 2007. We look to continue our success into a new Advanced Learning Centre to be opened in 2010. The school's website is www.dearnehigh.co.uk.

K.hempenall
x

To Carol
Love Amy x

Scott

J. cochlea

charlotte ef

Katie F

J.Neff
x

The Dearne High: A Specialist Humanities College

Out of the Shadows

Grosvenor House Publishing Limited

Grosvenor House
Publishing Limited

First published in 2008
by Grosvenor House Publishing Limited
Crossweys
28 - 30 High Street
Guildford
Surrey
GU1 3HY

Typeset by Grosvenor House Publishing Limited

The Dearne High and individually named students' rights to be identified as
authors of this book has been asserted in accordance with section 77 of the
Copyright, Designs and Patents Act, 1988

All characters in this publication are fictitious and any resemblance to real
persons, living or dead, is purely coincidental.

We are very grateful to Mark Denton and Joan Townend for granting us
permission to use their photographs in this book:

'A Panoramic of Magical Mirrors,' 'Graham Taylor and Dearne students,'
'Conisbrough Castle,' 'Tantallon,' 'Ancient Oaks,' 'Alnwick,' 'Golitha,'
'Chalk-Cliff,' 'Sycamore,' 'Tinmines,' and 'Signed copies of Tersias'

A CIP record for this book
is available from the British Library

ISBN 978-1-906645-28-1

Dedication

We are proud and delighted to present our College's first fully endorsed and professional publication. *Out of the Shadows* is a collection of unique stories written for young people by young people. Students at the Dearne High have written these stories to portray everything around us in a way that only children can truly express. The creation of this book was very special for all of us and we hope that everyone who reads these stories experiences the same sense of discernment for light, dark and shades of grey, as we did...

As a community we are striving to fully embrace a humanitarian approach to education where creativity and risk taking feature largely in the pursuit of excellence. We hope to demonstrate this evolving ethos within every page of *Out of the Shadows*. This book is consequently dedicated to all 'Dearne learners' of the past, present and future, as we collectively strive to develop a fully inclusive college where Every Child really does Matter.

Mr. Neil Clark
Headteacher

Miss Bethany Pickering
Y7 student

"A panoramic of magical mirrors glints towards the tantalising opportunities of the future. A parallel line of benches seat invisible students and guides ready to walk away from a previously regimented and straight- line viewpoint. Grey shadows hint towards clear fields and clean skies that are the magic of the moment and our future.

Oracles whisper that dynamic and innovative architecture will soon define the outline of a more interesting and challenging horizon. Minstrels sing of how altered forms of light and shadow will inspire our senses to transform learning for the better. Whilst no one can truly predict the future, I am sure they are right. The reflective light of the Dearne High will shine even stronger, as future structures alter the shadows of a continually evolving landscape.

'A Panoramic of Magical Mirrors' by Mark Denton, 2008.

In true Humanitarian spirit, we guide a multitude of brave young souls who fool their shadows by generating the light of improvement from within. They are as ready for new visions, battles and victories as they are for older ones. Just like adults they can reject their silhouettes whenever they want to, step out of the shadows and accept the consequences of 'all light,' or 'all dark.' Sadly, none but the most learned, or magical alter hasty decisions and true raw diamonds are harder to find than shape nowadays...

We are therefore fortunate that a deeper magic can make near perfect shades of youth. Indeed, there is nothing more alluring for a young writer than the precise blackness of ink juxtaposed against the pristine whiteness of a published page. Furthermore it could also be said that the wisest of souls share wisdom through the lightest of touches..."

Anonymous.

Acknowledgements

Many visitors to our school have commented on the special uniqueness of what we offer our children. It is often the support of these visitors that helps us travel that extra mile. High profile Yorkshire people have been very helpful in promoting our distinctly humanitarian and progressive ethos. Several of these were particularly powerful in that their visits inspired the production of this book.

Out of the Shadows would not have been possible were it not for the unstinting kindness that Graham Taylor, (author of *Shadowmancer*) showed to our students and college. He provided a day's services for free and donated a series of books that served to inspire our students to become authors. The majority of the stories in this book fall within the fantasy genre, of which Graham Taylor is a true master. Many of the original ideas for these stories came from tips and encouragement offered to individuals by Graham throughout his visit.

Thanks go to all the staff involved in supporting the students with their stories and creating and marketing this book afterwards. These included: Mr. Clark, Mrs. Crichton, Mrs. Tivey, Miss Wilmot, Mrs. Rhodes, Mr. Slassor, Miss Gamble, Mr. Child, Mr. Stretton, Miss Thompson, Miss Ibbotson, Miss Timms, Mr. Ward and Mrs. Townend.

Further to Graham's visit, Mark Denton offered a series of photography talks and landscape photographs to our students as further inspiration for their work. Better still, he even allowed us to reproduce some of his most recent pictures to complement several individual stories throughout *Out of the Shadows*. His inspirational landscapes capture the perfect transition between light, dark and shades of grey. Many of our stories are based on these contrasts and an understanding that few people truly experience the ability, or desire, to walk out of the shadows.

Nick Toczek and Brian Blessed also helped us with the publication of this book. We are extremely grateful for this. Nick Toczek (author of a multitude of collaborative texts including *Read Me Out Loud*) worked with our students on their description of the book as a whole and helped discuss the project as a business venture. Brian Blessed was delighted to read a draft of the text and responded with typical charismatic and positive gusto about the quality of the work from his 'old school.'

I would also like to offer a very special thank you to the Specialist Schools and Academies Trust and in particular Jacqueline Anthony and Philippa Darley, who are responsible for the progress of the one hundred and eighty Humanities Colleges, for supporting this initiative. Without their funding and support the professional production of this book and more importantly the specialist ethos of the college as a whole would not have been possible.

Finally no acknowledgements in any publication would be complete without offering thanks to the world's most prolific and successful author 'Anonymous.' We were absolutely delighted that 'Anonymous' wrote a piece of fantasy prose specifically for us. *Out of the Shadows* not only inspired Mark Denton's *A Panoramic Of Magical Mirrors*, it went on to become the title for this anthology!

So to summarise - positive people and role models are the true architects of our constructive changes and development. They do make a difference! Without them, we would never emerge from any of our shadows. It is true to say that very successful people often leave other people feeling left in the shadows. I personally believe however that truly successful people usually bring others out of the shadows. This is also the privilege of teaching.

The perfectly formed silhouettes that metamorphose regularly between our current old building and our new design now jump with a new found glee. Shining with a pure inner brilliance, our children will soon walk within even greener fields and under bluer skies. I look forward to the day that this is commonplace. I hope that the publication of this book helps us take a further step out of the shadows towards the new horizons that await...

Mr. Peter Shaw
Assistant Headteacher

Endorsements from those involved in this book's production.

GRAHAM TAYLOR:
"It is highly exciting to see such a piece of creative literature as this. Dearne High has pulled out all the stops to make this book a great read. I am sure that many of the young and inspired writers will go on to even greater things in the future."

NICK TOCZEK:
"I've worked in more than 4,000 schools, many of them challenging and demanding, but am truly impressed with Dearne. There is a real focus on giving the pupils a clear sense of their own value. It's there in the technology that they can access and in the way they are treated individually. More importantly, however, it's there in what they're taught and how they're taught.

This book is a shining example of what that empowering ethos can produce. I know of many schools that have published small collections of work by pupils, but none that have done so in a fully professional manner. This isn't just another cheaply printed pamphlet for parents to buy, it's a real book compiled and created by the pupils and staff as a proper business venture. Like so many of the projects that Dearne offers to its pupils, the production of this anthology has given each participating pupil a taste of the world of work.

From the mature and interesting writing in here to the quality of the finished product, this book is proof that the school is giving the pupils skills and experience that go way beyond mere exam grades.

Furthermore, it greatly increases their self-confidence, broadens their horizons and gives them a real sense of achievement... oh, and it's a good book too, so read and enjoy it!"

BRIAN BLESSED:

"*This book is absolutely sensational! A great example of imaginative fiction. Consummate balance of adventure, skilled characterisation, novelty of storyline and adept use of fantasy themes. It is a wonderful team effort, involving students and teachers alike at the Dearne High, Goldthorpe!! To top it all, would you believe it, this is the school I attended in the late forties and fifties. It was an inspiration then, and an inspiration now! My childhood was so blissfully happy that even today the same jolly DNA molecules of my infancy dance about together with frolicsome fizz! And that's exactly the effect this amazing book has on me. It makes me want to filch a lollipop from the fridge and read it all over again. I see fine futures for all the students involved. There is plenty for everyone's taste here. It is a tour-de-force! A staggering achievement, congratulations! It is a privilege to contribute to the foreword.*"

JACQUELINE ANTHONY / PHILIPPA DARLEY:

"*Dearne High's new publication, Out of the Shadows, is an excellent example of how humanities colleges can develop innovative applied learning for their students. Written by students, for students, with the guidance of a professional author, the project has provided opportunities to develop many skills young people need for the real world of work and higher education. The publication celebrates the outward looking school that seeks to make the most of its students' intellectual capacity. And the students have written some great stories too!*"

Mark Denton:
"Never lose sight of how beautiful your county is. It is always your home. Pictures speak a thousand words. Enjoy them!"

'Conisbrough Castle – Mark Denton, 2008'

Contents

CONTENTS

'Tantallon' by Mark Denton, 2008

"A once fine looking castle now looked derelict. Shadows spread over its unchecked face, windows were boarded and tiles were missing from the roof."

Taken

A once fine looking castle now looked dark, gloomy and derelict. Shadows spread over its unchecked face, windows were boarded and tiles were missing from the roof. The rooms inside were damp and cobwebs hung from the ceiling. The wooden floorboards were all rotten and eroded whilst the walls embroidered with beautifully illustrated images were ruined and made no sense.

There was a room that stood out from the rest. The dining room was situated in the middle of the castle. Huge stone pillars towered over the two people that remained rooted to the spot in the middle of the room. Pools of dirty, unclear, foul water surrounded them everyway they turned. Their eyes were full of fear and fixed upon the three hooded figures before them, raised on the set of eroded steps.

In the darkest, murkiest corner lay Monya, hunched over and crying, fright etched all over her face. Her whimpering could be heard throughout the whole castle, ricocheting off the walls. The putrid smell of gas rose like mist in a churchyard, weaving its way in and out, occupying every available space.

A warm breeze floated in through the open windows of the Bakery's Legs, as face after face smiled widely at the little 8-year-old girl sat in front of them, little Monya, the chosen one, the 'key' to the 'other world'.

A bell sounded through the room, everyone fell silent. It was time to crown Monya. She sat on the raised platform waiting for that fateful moment, when she would become the most important person in the magical world.

"*Monya Cainey, you have been chosen to be the protector of the other world, your job is to protect all from all evil and to protect us from them! So therefore, I proclaim you the key to the other world!*" the old wizard shouted.

Cheers erupted all around, people were singing loudly and drinking to their hearts galore, and generally everyone was having fun.

This memory seemed like a lifetime away, as Monya lay there hunched up, the tune of an early bird could be heard faintly in the distance. Alexa and Coby stood there not taking their eyes of the hooded Gryffclaws. You could see the coggs moving inside Alexa's head, trying to figure out what to do. Coby set off at a sprint towards where Monya lay. Beneath one of the dirty hoods, a mouth with big yellow teeth and a huge tongue could be seen as it muttered words of an incantation and Coby was hoisted into mid-air. An ear-splitting scream sounded through the castle, bouncing off the fragile stones, as Coby slammed against the wall, he fell to the floor and lay there motionless.

Alexa span around. Rage disguised her usual pretty features. She raised her hands and pointed at the ugly hooded Gryffclaw in the middle. A gash revealed itself as the hood fell from the creature's face. The creature was a mixture of hunchback and hedgehog, as liquid poured down its face.

The castle illuminated brightly as a Gryffclaw conjured a power ball from its scaly hands and sent it soaring through the air, aiming at Alexa. Alexa dived to the left and rolled behind a pillar. The power ball crashed into the same wall as Coby. The wall came crashing down around Coby, narrowly missing him. With great difficulty he lifted himself onto all fours and pushed himself to his feet. He wiped off the dust that had settled onto his clothes and in his hair, then shot a green jet of light flying towards the Gryffclaws, joining in with Alexa, whose hands were moving so fast it was a blur. Jets of light were bouncing around the room, sending parts of the room falling to the floor. Coby closed his eyes and breathed in deeply as his feet levitated off the floor. He spun round in mid-air and sent a wave of cold air spiralling through the room, knocking the three Gryffclaws off their feet. Alexa and Coby took their chance and started firing spells at them yet again. A jet of light hit the closest Gryffclaw right in the chest, a wave of shock ran through its body before it died. The two remaining Gryffclaws joined hands as the two youngsters high fived.

"*Arma sa ta!*" the Gryffclaws' husky voices rang shrilly. The ceiling started to cave in. Monya sat in the corner huddling her knees, wishing to be in a place were there wasn't magic, where no one knew her, where there were no big monsters.

The ground fell from beneath them. Alexa and Coby looked at each other confusion blinding them. They were spinning around and around. There was a shriek of excruciating pain as the two worlds collided and the two remaining Gryffclaws were shredded into a thousand pieces.

Flashes of foreign cities and towns could be seen, alongside people walking down the streets, and snatches of conversations could be heard. Fresh air filled their lungs. They were falling, their feet finally finding solid ground. Screams and shouts could be heard everywhere. Well it's not every day that two young adults and a dirty little girl appear out of nowhere is it?

Alexa looked around, faces were staring at them. She walked up to the nearest man who was wearing a pinstriped suit.

"Excuse me sir, could you tell me where I am please?" she questioned.

"Why, you're in London, little lady."

"And where exactly is London?"

"It's in England. Are you alright?" the man asked sounding concerned.

"Yes, yes, thank you."

Alexa turned round to Coby and Monya, 'the non-magical world' she mouthed to them both.

Coby took hold of Monya's grubby hand and the three of them marched down the street, having no idea where they were going. They turned left into an empty street. They entered a café, that they were sure plenty of people would never dare step foot in. The door chimed when it opened. They were the only customers apart from an old insane man in his late 80's sat on the table closest to the window. He was muttering in a strange language to himself.

Alexa sat at the table furthest away from him scared of being caught up in his madness. Gazing at a canvas picture of green fields hanging on the wall, Alexa sighed, a miserable sigh.

"So, any ideas how we ended up here then?" Coby asked, staring at Alexa intently.

"No idea!" she replied, frustration clear in her voice. *"What are we going to do now? We've got nowhere to sleep, no food, and no money. I mean look at little Monya. We can hardly walk her round the street looking like that,"* Alexa said in a hushed tone. She grabbed Monya's hand and gave it a sympathetic squeeze, then plastered a fake smile on her face not wanting to worry Monya. She stared intensely into those beautiful ocean blue eyes, she could lose herself in those forever. She realised she had stared for too long, and quickly turned away, her cheeks blooming pink, an awkward silence followed, Monya was the first to break the silence.

"Can we go home, please? I'm tired." She rubbed her eyes and yawned lazily.

"Sweetie, if we knew how we would," Coby simpered.

"Hey," he looked at Alexa. *"Lighten up, how about we go find a place to sleep for tonight then we'll sort everything out tomorrow, what do you say, huh?"*

"Let's go!" Alexa plastered on her dazzling smile and everyone got to their feet. Coby knew they would be needing money, so he changed the big coins in his pockets to £50 notes. He flashed them in front of Alexa's face.

"This way we can get a decent night's kip, in one of those fancy hotels and even fill our stomachs with the best food the next food shop can offer."

The Star of Jhansi was a small Indian restaurant with glittering lights in the window and sets of silver tables and chairs sat outside in the last hour of the glowing sunset. There was a warm breeze that floated through the air.

Monya sniffed appreciatively and went and sat at one of the outside tables. Alexa watched Coby strut over and sit next to Monya, his sandy hair flopping over his face, giving him a hot, surfer look. Alexa joined them. She picked up one of the fancy menus that lay on the table. She gawked at it. She had never heard of any of this food, Rogan Josh, Naan bread, Chicken Tikka Masala. Coby picked a random thing and ordered it for them all to share. A waiter came and took their order then melted away.

They sat chatting about how different London looked to Little Vangley, with all the busy shops, big bridges and beautiful restaurants. The waiter placed a stainless steel dish on the table. He lifted off the lid.

"*Chicken korma,*" he announced. "*Hope you enjoy your food and your night.*"

"*Thanks,*" everyone said gratefully and smiling. Coby dished out the curry and they all ate as if they had been starved for a week. Alexa placed a £20 note on the table and they left, their stomachs full, their spirits high but their bodies aching with tiredness.

They stopped a woman in the street and asked where the nearest hotel was.

"*Oh, it's just down Kingston Street.*" They looked at her with a puzzled look on their faces.
The woman laughed.

"*Turn left at that street there, then right and right again.*"

"*Thank you!*" they bellowed down the street, as they made their way to a good night's rest. They didn't realise that they were outside the Tower Hotel. They opened the

10

big oak doors and stood in the entrance hall, staring around in awe.

The floors were marble white, the reception desk matching the floor but decorated with golden detail. The central staircase was huge and spiralled around the hotel, the steps were marble and the lights were dimmed as everyone bathed in a simmering shine.

Coby walked up to the reception desk. The woman behind the desk had a sweet smile on her face that said I wish I wasn't here.

"*Hello, welcome to the Tower Hotel.*"

"*Um, hey, could I book a room for three, just for tonight please.*"

The receptionist handed Coby a set of keys, "*third floor, and second door to the left.*"

"*Thanks,*" Alexa said. They set off up the stairs and made their way to their room. They finally found it, opened the door and flopped on the three single beds. The room was gorgeous with cream walls and chocolate silk bed sheets.

"*I wonder if we're ever going to get out of here?*" Alexa sighed.

"*Sure we are,*" said Coby cheerily.

They all lay back and fell into a well-earned sleep.

Leah Cook

Death Incarnate

The screams and shouts of my warriors echoed around me. After all, I was Emperor Talen, master of all evil (or so they thought) the one everyone feared. I had fought many wars that had led to me vanquishing almost every tribe in the area. The only one I didn't own was Kayleb's. He was my equal and I couldn't defeat him. Even if my warriors were the best they could be it still wouldn't happen. I desperately wanted to win for Leah, to show her I was better than Kayleb.

Kayleb and I had been rivals since childhood. We had fought for Leah and he had won so they married and I was left alone. From what everyone saw they were happy but behind closed doors they argued and in the end she left him. Three weeks after this a war broke out between us. Kayleb blamed me for Leah leaving him, but I didn't know where she was. Kayleb thwarted my warriors and I, leaving me distraught and ready to give up on everything.

Leah found me after four long years of searching. She helped me restore myself and soon I was out fighting. I soon became leader of most tribes, but once Kayleb found out about us he went crazy and came to look for me. Kayleb challenged me to a full-on war where whoever won gained control of the other's land. I agreed but still had my doubts.

Looking down from the hilltop I smiled. His warriors were dying fast, whereas mine were becoming stronger. I watched an eagle fly over the heads of the living, as happy as I could have been, when suddenly a large black object came at me from the other side of the battlefield. I tried to dodge it but failed miserably. Kayleb had killed me. It was over. I was dead, gone forever...

Although I was dead the fight still carried on around me. My warriors kept trying but in the end they lost to his powers. Many of them died and those who remained fled not in anger but in fear, without me they were useless. Leah searched for me through the night tears pouring down her freckled face, she felt a sharp pain in her jaw and two of her teeth began to grow, razor sharp and shining in the moonlight.

"Not now, please not now," she murmured. Suddenly she had a thirst for blood, but she pushed it aside to carry on looking for me. When she found me she bit into my neck, ripping the flesh from the bone, unable to restrain herself any longer.

"Oh no, what have I done?" Her eyes grew wide as my eyes flickered open. She knelt at my side, her soft hand resting on mine.

"Goodbye Leah," I drew my last breath and closed my eyes slowly.

"Goodbye Talen, my love." She closed her eyes, turned and when she opened them a tomb stood before her. Engravings around the sides showed certain aspects of my life.

"Your final resting place," Leah said, as she laid my body down inside. *"I will join you soon."* She engraved these words beside me:

"My love, my darling, forever you will be in my heart."

Then she left sealing the tomb behind her.

I woke staring up at the cobwebbed ceiling. There was a layer of dust over my body, like a dirty blanket protecting me from the thick air. I made to stand up, but to my surprise, I saw Leah laying there her mouth slightly open. Her body wasn't dusty like mine, but clean like she was taking a nap on a normal day. I walked over to her body, bent down and kissed her on the lips. A silvery vapour rose from her mouth. It formed a face that said, "*Welcome,*" then disappeared. I walked wearily to the door that was covered in spiders. With a little push it opened to reveal an ancient graveyard full of my dead warriors. I walked down row after row occasionally looking down at a name. At the end of one of the rows stood a tall man. He wore a long leather coat and a hat that covered his face.

· "*Welcome back emperor. Did you enjoy your sleep? I certainly did, but it's nice to feel the sun on your face, don't you think? Well down to business. You are now here in the 21st century. It is more advanced than you might think, a lot of things have changed, as you will soon realise. You don't truly exist so don't worry about little things like housing and money - we have those things ready for you; by the way - Leah will help you when you need it, she will be your guide. All I am here for is to tell you what is going on. I'm lord Salem by the way - Leah's father. I am very glad she left Kayleb for you. He was horrible. She killed herself you know, a few months after you died. She obviously couldn't live without you. What else have I got to mention, oh yeah your house is just to the left of that gate over there. Can you see it? Yes? Okay, I must get going, but one last thing, I know you're good at 'directing,' but you might need 'HELP.' You will understand soon enough.*" His voice began to fade and his body blurred. *"Good luck,"* he said, before disappearing completely.

The chirping of a bird woke me early the next morning. The traffic hadn't yet started, so all I could hear was that one bird singing its song to the world, but the peacefulness didn't last long. Soon the streets outside were full of taxis, motorbikes and cars, emitting gases into the once happy world. I changed, then decided to brave the streets of New York City. Once I was out there, it wasn't too bad, buildings towered over me touching the sky, streets lined with shops and work offices spiralled around the city. Soon I saw a magnificent sight. It was the tallest building for miles around and cast a shadow on those around it. I joined a small group of people and walked inside. We clamoured into a lift that set off upwards. Most of the people had left by the time we reached the top floor. There was only an elderly woman with grey hair and me. We stepped out of the lift to see a wondrous sight. The walls were made entirely of glass, showing a spectacular view of New York. The carpet was a pale yellow and several lamps cast an odd glow over the room. In the corner sat a young girl around the age of eight. Giant tears splashed down her thin and hollow face and onto her skinny arm. I walked towards her but she jumped up and ran to the other side of the room.

"It's okay, I'm not going to hurt you, I just want to help," I said. She looked at me suspiciously, but didn't run off as I edged towards her. *"My name is Talen. What's yours?"* She took a deep breath then said,

"S-S-Sophie, my dad has l-left me here, he k-k-killed my mom then brought me here, I don't k-know where I am you see. I'm from New Zealand. He wouldn't f-feed

me and he hit me. I'm scared h-he'll come back and k-kill me like he did m-mom, will you h-help me?" I looked into her blue eyes. Her face was red and puffy and her lip quivered. Then she flew into my arms and her tears splashed on my chest.

"Of course you can come with me. My house is a few blocks from here. We can get something to eat on our way there. Would you like that?" I patted her back sympathetically.

"Y-yes sir I would l-like that, thank you sir." She took my hand and led me towards the door.

In the weeks that followed I opened my heart more and more to Sophie, telling her about Leah, the war and how I was there, but at night I had dreams that told me not to trust her, that she was evil, that she was trying to stop me doing the things I needed to do. I was scared and didn't know what to. Should I trust her or trust my dreams? She cried when I tried leaving the house and she cried when I wouldn't play with her. My suspicion grew stronger every day and the stronger it got the less I talked to her. She began to shout at me telling me I was horrible to her and that she wished she were back with her dad in New Zealand. I woke up one morning and she was gone. She wasn't asleep and she wasn't playing in the garden. She wasn't anywhere. Was it my fault or had she been taken? I worried about her for a few days, but then realised she was probably happier without me.

I looked for jobs hoping that was what I needed to do. I worked at a cafe, a supermarket, a clothes shop and a perfume shop, each of which I got fired from. I kept seeing a girl with red hair who looked strangely familiar. She worked at the café, and visited the other shops that

I worked at. She smiled but never talked which was starting to get a little annoying. I was walking home from yet another job when I heard an ear piercing scream coming from down an ally way. I ran towards it wondering what was happening. Unexpectedly I saw Sophie and the redheaded girl glaring at each other in the darkness. It wasn't until then that I realised who it was.

"*Leah!*" She held out her hand signalling silence.

"*Be quiet Talen, I'm having a little conversation with Sophia. She tried to stop you succeeding. Lucky I was here really. You told her too much. It's dangerous you know taking in little girls like this. Who sent you here Sophia? Was it Kayleb?*" She smiled as if she was playing a silly game with a school friend. "*Oh, not going to answer are we? I'll just have to kill you now won't I?*" She pointed her index finger at Sophie. A shot of orange light flew out it. The light hit her heart making her scream again. She burst into flames then disappeared.

"*Yes Talen it is me, I have been watching over you, protecting you, Sophia - or as you know her, Sophie - was Kayleb's servant, she did whatever he told her to do. She must have been waiting for all these years, just to stop you. How she found out I do not know and for now I must go.*" Her voice was trailing away just like Salem's had. Her outline was also becoming blurred, "*Good luck!*"

> '*Congratulations, you are a winner!!!*
> *If you accept you will be Directing a*
> *Brand new show called HELP,*
> *You, along with two others will*
> *Be helping Alan Brook Produce*
> *The show, Auditions start tomorrow*
> *At 5pm, Please arrive at the*

Premiere Theatre Before that time
If you have any problems please
Call this Number:
07854454674
Thank you,
Samantha Mallkurk'

That's what the letter said. I had no idea how they had got my address, but I wasn't complaining. I tried to remember something Salem had said to me.

"I know you're good at directing, but you might need HELP," is what he meant. It had to be and there was nothing else! I walked into the theatre expecting to see something spectacular, but all I saw was a hundred or so shabby seats gathered around a curved stage.

"This theatre definitely needs help," I muttered sarcastically. A voice sounded from the shadows –

"Welcome, you must be Talen. Leah is waiting back stage. We were ready to start, but we had to wait for you didn't we? Come on now, hurry up now, we've wasted enough time!" He ushered me through a door to the right of the stage where, like he had said, Leah was waiting. She opened her mouth to say something, but the man interrupted.

"Sit down then. We don't have much time left. Now we need to do the parts of Helen, Tina, Lewis and Danny. Now that's better. Welcome everyone to the premiere of 'HELP.' Could you please take your seats ready for the show to start?"

Leah and I sat down ready on the front row, just as the voice had said. A babble of chatter filled the room but when the lights dimmed the room became silent, waiting.

"Danny, Danny where are you Danny?" shouted Tina searching the audience. *"I'm here mama don't worry I've been..."*

During the interval Alan beckoned us backstage with a worried look on his face.

"What?" Leah whispered angrily.

"There's a person, centre of the 3rd row. S/he's been chanting under their breath for about ten minutes now and things are starting to go wrong. Tina keeps being sick. Lewis has ripped his costume and Helen says she's forgotten her lines. Coincidence, I think not!" Alan commented. Leah peered to look at the person. She gasped then said –

"It's Sophia. Talen I will need your help to get rid of her. This is the only thing that will kill her. My last spell obviously didn't work and this is the only alternative. We just need to wait until the right moment!" They started again and everything seemed to be going well until Helen screamed. Blood was pouring from her chest and onto the floor. To my horror, Sophia was walking over the heads of the crowd to the stage, which by now was covered in blood.

"Now Talen, we need to go now," she grabbed my arm and we ran onstage...

"Stop, STOP! Everyone stop, sit down. All of you, you're OK, just listen to me," said Leah bravely. *"This beast is not from our land. It is a demon, worse than the devil and only one thing can stop it - the power of love. This demon fears love so that's what we need to do. LOVE people - come on, think of your families, your lovers, anyone who you love, it's not hard look!"* She turned and kissed me. Not a tiny peck on the cheek, a proper kiss on the lips. My body began to tingle as we

rose upwards. When we stopped kissing, we stayed in the air and watched Sophia thrash around in pain.

"*No, no, don't do this, stop it! I haven't done anything, noooooo!*" She disappeared again, this time leaving a layer of green smoke behind her. We kissed again and this time it felt as if we were being pushed through a tight hole. I fell to the floor feeling something hard cut into my hand. I looked to see what it was and there was Kayleb lying dead at my side. There was a deep cut across his neck. Gradually the fight around us died away. Finally I was free to marry Leah...

"*Do you Leah Eloise Forrest take Talen Sage Harrison to be your lawful wedded husband?*"

"*I Do!*"

"*Do you Talen Sage Harrison take Leah Eloise Forrest to be your lawful wedded wife?*"

"*I Do!*"

"*I now pronounce you Man and Wife.*"

Kayleigh Webster and Liam Bailey.

turned a pale green, then lime green, as all his anger and hate for the foul creatures was transferred to his blade. Regnar had roared,

"You will pay for what you have done!" As the words left his mouth the goblins had charged screeching and laughing. Regnar had laughed and run at them, his shield as big as himself crunched against the beasts. Then he had bellowed

"Kaldain my brother run while you have breath in your lungs for I will kill these worms!"

Kaldain didn't want to leave but he knew when Regnar was serious, he didn't mean to play around, he meant to get out.

"I shall tell tales of your bravery brother and your valour, farewell may Shaklog be with you," bellowed Kaldain sprinting as fast as he could.

Kaldain had run until his lungs felt dry and would not move. He had come so close to finding the spoils and riches of Skukruk, that it was something that was always on his mind as well as losing two of his closest friends. He ran and ran down corridors and through rooms for two weeks then he heard voices; they were muffled but far two strange to be that of a human being. Kaldain clutched the handle and started to turn it but to his horror, the door was pulled from the other side. There stood a troll a tall ugly thing with skin that didn't fit its body properly. It had scars on its head; its skin was mouldy and burnt. The armour it wore was badly cracked and had parts missing. A rusty dagger was stuck in its shoulder and had been there for some time. It slavered as it looked docilely at Kaldain figuring out what to make of him.

He was frozen to the spot, and then Kaldain started to run as fast as he could. He could hear its large feet slapping the floor behind him. Suddenly a strange twanging noise met Kaldain's ears. He turned slowly and there stood the troll with a loaded bow in its hands, its deformed fingers released the bow string ...A piercing sharp pain went through Kaldain's left leg. He looked down in agony. There it was, a hand crafted arrow, exposing the bone. Kaldain gave out a yelp and snapped the wooden shaft, but the arrow point was still stuck in his flesh. Kaldain unsheathed his blade and attempted to walk over to the troll. It looked worried at this so loaded another arrow and released it into Kaldain's right leg. Kaldain collapsed to the floor as the pain shot up his leg.

"Arghh!"

The troll gave out an evil laugh, then kept smirking; thinking it could finish him off any time. It made its way over to him still smirking. Kaldain picked his sword up and swung it frantically at the troll. Blood squirted into Kaldain's face as the troll moaned and started to sway forwards and backwards then it keeled over next to Kaldain. The dagger that had been embedded in its shoulder pinged out and stuck into his chest. All went black...

Kaldain awoke to find the troll's head above his own. He lay still for a moment wondering what to do. The troll had a gash in its leg stretching from its thigh to its hip, it stared at him with blood still running down its leg. Kaldain didn't understand how the dagger had just been inches away from his heart and had made mincemeat of his armour. Kaldain started to crawl away. He knew the noise and the body plus the blood would attract gnolls.

These beasts were humanoid, but half hyena and were scavengers so blood and bodies were a bonus.

He was in excruciating pain but had to go on as he could already hear the gnolls howling not far from where he was. Kaldain started crawling, on and on... He thought he had been going on for hours, but had only been going about twenty minutes. Then he discovered a beam of light that hurt his eyes. He couldn't believe it. He had found a way out, but giant rocks blocked most of the exit. His only hope was to move the rocks, but he could not stand because of the excruciating pain in his legs not to mention his chest. His wounds were wide open and blood trailed behind him, which had attracted the attention of a gnoll scouting party. The gnoll barked to its pack. They followed, looking at him, waiting for any sudden movement, as they liked to toy and kill their prey. Kaldain moved his arm in an attempt to clear a rock. He turned his head slightly and in the corner of his eye he saw the group and screamed. Kaldain knew his end was near. He didn't want it to be over, but knew there was nothing he could do. They snarled and ran at him swinging their blades and axes straight for his head. Then he was in darkness. He felt his soul lifting out from within him then he became light and entered the spirit world. There was a chilly breeze that seemed to grasp his whole body before his eyes and his whole life started flickering before him...

Andrew Daniels

A Paladin's Quest

Along time ago in the medieval era a child had been born with the mark of Zarthus. Zarthus was the leader of the holy crusaders also known as Paladins who rid the land of evil. This child's fate was the most important one out of all the Paladins born. They named him Valen. One day he would save the entire land but at a deadly cost. His father was killed three years after the child's birth. As a child Valen was told of the tale of the god demon Dradoth. Then he was told how Dradoth was supposedly connected to the black temple to the north, but did not actually live there because he had his own realm. Another darker tale was that any person who braved the challenges of the black temple would receive the honour of challenging the god demon himself. This is Valen's story.

It had been thirty years since Valen's birth and he had become a mighty Paladin. Valen was a strong man with hair as black as night. He had a look in his eyes, which made his enemies fear him. Valen lived in his hometown of Orgish. Valen was known for some amazing triumphant battles like those against the dragon of Grogash and the undead of bloodpath cave. All the kings and queens summoned him when they had a threat to their land. The head guard of the kingdom of Ruthorne called Valen to come and see the king. Valen set off to see the king and from that point on his life would never be the same again.

After arriving at the kingdom the king greeted him and gave Valen orders to kill some Boliwogs to the east.

Valen said he would come back the next day and slay the beasts. Valen set off back to Orgish on his beautiful horse Thunderbolt. She had short black hair and red eyes, which gleamed like rubies implanted in her eye sockets.

Thunderbolt was as tough as a dreaded ogre and faster than anything roaming the land. Valen set off on Thunderbolt and was nearly back at Orgish when he saw the worst thing he had ever seen in his life. Orgish was on fire!

He got off Thunderbolt and ran into Orgish. Everyone was dead apart from the leader who walked towards Valen, but he was very weak. He collapsed onto Valen and Valen laid him on the floor.

"He...came and...destroyed everything...travel to...the black temple...to the north...Valen... and... kill...Dradoth."

Dradoth was the tale from his childhood. Valen was angry at the death of his village and vowed revenge. The heat of the blaze began to sweep over Valen like magma infused with the wind. The smell of rotting corpses was sickening and the debris of the town was a painful sight to see. Then he saw a shadowy figure to the north. It was a big shadow with amazing wings. He couldn't see exactly what it was because of the smoke.

It was time for Valen to do what he was destined to do since he was born. He got on Thunderbolt and set off to the black temple. When he arrived he took a good look at it. It was a large temple that went underground. It had big black spikes on top capable of piercing the strongest armour. It was a place of sadness, evil and death. The sky became red, as he got closer to the entrance. Valen went into the entrance and began to descend some stairs. The further down he got the more evil a presence there seemed to be. He got to the bottom and five werewolves were stood there. Their fur was blacker than Dradoth's heart. Blood dripped from their fangs and their eyes gleamed white like diamonds. They then looked at Valen. They started to show their fangs and growled.

Then in a split second they all started attacking Valen, but he dodged them and began to stab at them all. A werewolf almost pierced its claw into Valen's heart, but Valen stabbed it before it got him. Valen killed four werewolves and one remained. Then after seeing his fellow werewolves' deaths he went into blood craze. This was when a werewolf got really angry and became extreme. The werewolf ran into the next room. Valen ran after it and then he saw standing before him a massive ogre. This ogre was bigger than five men standing on each other. Valen ran with all his might and stabbed the fierce green ogre in its leg. The ogre swept with its huge club at Valen's head almost knocking it off. Valen used his shield to block it and the ogre hit the werewolf instead knocking its head off, but Valen's shield was destroyed after taking such heavy damage. Valen was now defenceless.

Valen ran around looking for a weak spot. He saw that the skin where the ogre's heart was, looked a lot weaker than the rest of his skin. Valen ran wildly and used his sword to stab into the ogre pulling himself up as he did.

He stabbed and pulled himself up in the ogre till he got to the heart. Then the Paladin lunged his sword into the ogre's heart piercing it until the ogre fell with a deafening roar. Then Valen saw what he had been looking for. A large door with ancient text above which said 'Citadel Chamber.' This was it. Valen had braved the nightmare of the black temple and earned the right to challenge the god demon Dradoth to a duel.

Valen pulled a lever opening the door. He entered the room and there was.........no one. He was expecting Dradoth to be there, but it was just a room with dusty spell books and a bed. It must have been where Dradoth's followers rested. Then Valen noticed a shrine in the room. There was a book open on the floor with the spell written in ancient text that said 'Summon The Lord.' Valen prepared himself and summoned 'The Lord.' There before him, stood Dradoth himself who shouted –

"Who dares summon me from my realm?!!" Dradoth was a large black demon with horns as sharp as any blade. His skin was a blood coloured red and 10 times tougher than any armour. His wings were as big as his body and they were so sharp, they could cut through almost anything. His sword was gleaming as bight as the sun because it was the legendary blazing sword. Many warriors sought out this blade because of its beauty and power. They all challenged Dradoth, but all falling to the very sword they were trying to take.

"You there! Are you one of my followers? I told you not to summon me! No...wait...You're a Paladin...I knew one day you would come and try to kill me just like your father did. That's right I killed your father. What a fool he was. Never mind though, you will be with him

soon." All this time in Valen's life he had never known how his father died. Valen readied himself for a fight and whispered to himself -

"*May Zarthus protect me.*" Dradoth teleported them to an arena within his realm. Then it began.

Dradoth charged at Valen and Valen charged at Dradoth. Then swords clashed together.

"*You're as useless as your father,*" shouted Dradoth. Then after being reminded about his father's death the rage in Valen exploded and he went crazy slashing at Dradoth. He forced Dradoth backwards and attacked Dradoth's legs. Then Valen ran and climbed up the fence on the outer ring of the arena and jumped onto Dradoth's back. He pulled himself onto his head and stabbed Dradoth's eye. Then the demon grabbed Valen and flung him at the wall. That one hit made Valen lose his sword and now he had no weapon. Valen ran up to Dradoth, but Dradoth used his blazing sword and slashed Valen, causing his leg to be mortally wounded. Dradoth began walking to Valen slowly.

"*You lost, Valen and it looks like you won't be joining your father after all, because when you die your spirit will be tortured forever in my realm!*" It seemed like it was all going to end. Blood began to flow out of Valen's leg like a river. No weapon. No shield. No way to move. Defenceless. Valen had been defeated.

Dradoth began to walk to Valen ready to rip his heart out with his bare hands. Just at that moment Valen remembered the divine aura spell. Paladins only knew this spell and it came at a great cost. The curse if using the spell was death to the caster, but the good thing was that it blasted the entire land with Holy Spirit slaying any evil that crossed its path. Valen thought to himself, was this the end? Was there any other way? Dradoth got closer and closer to Valen. Valen decided this was the end. There was no other way.

Valen dragged himself to the middle of the arena and with his last burst of strength he managed to stand up even though his leg was cut deeply. Raising his arm in the air he shouted -

"Zarthus, smite this land!" Then Valen dropped dead on the floor. Dradoth looked at his corpse laughing at Valen thinking the spell had failed. Then above Valen's corpse a small flying yellow ball was hovering above him. Dradoth looked at it in confusion. Then in a split second the ball exploded sending a massive yellow magic cloud of dust flying through the air turning all Dradoth's minions to dust. Dradoth tried to resist it, but it was too powerful and Dradoth was pulled into the air. He didn't turn to dust, he just hovered in the air for a while.

Dradoth looked round. His realm was now colourful and there was no evil left at all. No undead guarding his castle, no spikes with human heads on them, no more of his influence. Then four vicious wolves appeared and ripped Dradoth apart...one arm here ...another leg there. The god demon Dradoth had been defeated. But what of his sword? The great Paladin god Zarthus destroyed it, forever. No more men would die for her beauty. The story of Valen was told to many people. It described how a brave and noble hero sacrificed himself for all the land. Of course to Valen, it wasn't a heroic thing. He did it for two reasons, to avenge his father and secondly to fulfil his purpose in life. He protected the land from evil.

Dominic Thompson

'Ancient Oaks' by Mark Denton, 2008

"The pink fluffy trees are like cotton candy. The light blue sky hasn't a cloud in sight, whilst the sunbeams fall brightly onto the glossy emerald grass like the scene from a newly painted picture."

Grace's Walk

Here I am walking through the bright, airy forest. The pink fluffy trees are like cotton candy. The light blue sky hasn't a cloud in sight, whilst the sunbeams fall brightly onto the glossy emerald grass like the scene from a newly painted picture. The fresh crisp air is all around me.

The once muddy path is now a walkway. As I walk down the golden pathway, the trees start to shake gently in the breeze. A pastel coloured rainbow shoots across the sky and the birds start to sing.

I feel as though I am in a whole new world. I start to walk and explore the grounds, as a little tiny leprechaun jumps out in front of me.

"*I've been sent here to look for you; my master is looking for you.*"

"*But who are you? And who's your master?*"

"*Master Candy, he's the candy maker down on Third Street.*"

"*Oh right,*" I reply in a puzzled voice.

"*We believe that you have a rare gem belonging to us.*"

"*My great grandmother's necklace?*"

"*Yes, now all you have to do is hand it over to Master Candy and he can power up the exclusive candy maker 4000.*"

"*I'm not handing over this necklace I've had it for over 10 years.*"

"*We can make all of the children in the world happy if you just hand it over.*"

"*Well when you put it like that, here you go.*"

The strange men fire up the candy maker 4000. They place the gem in the slot. The candy maker 4000 starts to produce all weird and wonderful sweets. Cherry and peach gums, apple and pineapple bonbons, grapefruit and mango jellies, chocolate and vanilla chocolate drops.

"Now Grace, we're going to have to ask you to leave as you can't see our next inventions."

They push me out through a door. I try to get back in, but the opening isn't there. I fall back and hit my head on the tree. My head starts spinning and I begin to see swirls. When I wake up, my head is no longer hurting. I realise that it is all just a strange dream.

Brittany Beighton

The Vampire Prophesy

My name is Jonas Okey; I live in Los Angeles, U.S.A. and
I'm 12 years old. I am originally from Doncaster, England,
but my family and I moved to give it a shot abroad. I am
going to tell you about an adventure that changed my life
and me forever. Read at your own risk.

Mrs. Mason was giving a lecture on Tectonic Plates in
double geography on a Thursday afternoon. Obviously I
wasn't paying attention, preferring to daydream and
wondering what I could do when I got home. I let my
mind wander. The work that Mrs. Mason had given us
was a crossword to find out specific words about geography, (which I didn't mind!) My Geography class is 'set
1.' Although I am in the top set for the majority of all my
classes, I don't really approve of the system. It's like an
intelligence meter that places thick ones at the bottom
and boffs at the top. It's not fair.

Inside my work booklet, was all my pat work, projects,
posters and pathetic handwriting! I am a whiz at puzzles
(guilty) so I decided to look through my past work. As I
explored through my less than best efforts, I found my
volcanoes poster and weather maps. My best work of the
academic year was based on the My World Sport mini
package. The sports annual I had designed, was filled with
facts, pictures and sports heroes, such as Cristiano
Ronaldo, Paula Radcliffe, Wayne Rooney, Tiger Woods...
and so on. As I looked through my masterpiece, a grey
note caught my eye eye. I hesitated to read it, not knowing what it was. I slipped it into my pocket and let the
thoughts of enquiry wander to the back of my mind.......

Mrs. Mason started to collect the finished work and told everyone to pack up their belongings and get ready for the bell. Year 7 is not as bad as I thought it was going to be, I knew that the first few weeks would be rough, but I knew I was going to fit in. We were only four weeks from our summer holidays. The year had gone really fast! The bell finally rang and the class swarmed out of the warm, dense room, before Mrs. Mason could assign homework. I didn't hesitate to join in the crowd. As I walked home, Lauren, Beth, Jake and I had to go past an ageing graveyard. My friends, especially Beth, loved the subsequent scary stuff! The local legend said that if you entered the graveyard for no reason in the month of December, you would get butchered by a madman with a chainsaw. So we all went for a walk at 8 o'clock on the first of December, as you do.

As we began to stroll more slowly home, I said goodbye to Jake, Lauren and Beth and they walked their separate routes home. I got home slightly earlier than normal. My mum Jackie and my dad Nickolas were working overtime at L.A.X Airport. I did my usual chores and then sat down and watched a little television. Then I remembered the note. I reached into my back trouser pocket and slowly took out the grey piece of paper. As I slowly opened the folds it spoke to me! I read its message aloud:

Graveyard
6 o'clock
Blue Bench
Don't be late
Signed: Your Destiny

I was shocked and dismayed that someone had decided to drop this one on me. I swore I would kill whoever had organised this likely prank, but I decided to go, no matter what. So I had a shower, got changed and wrote a note for my parents saying I was going out, when I would be in and that I had my mobile. (I actually told them that Jake had invited me for tea.) I had set off without telling them the truth and a sharp pain of guilt ran through my body. I remember thinking was this really a joke?

BATS AND GRAVESTONES

A branch snapped somewhere in the forest, I stopped dead still. Clouds sprinted across the night sky, eerily unravelling the eclipse in the mysterious maple sky and casting faint chocolate shadows on the mossy and cracked gravestones. I sat there waiting anxiously and quite scared and NOT ALONE...... Suddenly something moved in the undergrowth. I had been a complete idiot to agree such a meeting. Then, six large bats glided across the Maple Surface above..........

Then, the strangest thing happened. The bats, once black and leathery were now pink and fleshy. A middle - aged man, an elderly woman, a teenage girl and a toddler boy appeared before me. They stared; I started to panic and to run. They caught me in a short period of time and transformed back into the black beasts carrying me away...

I felt as if I was falling to the black road below me, but the four freaky family members were holding me tight. After a while my arms started to hurt so much I thought I was going to be detached from them and plummet to the ground below. The moon had never looked so big or detailed before; it was mysterious, but beautiful. Eventually we landed (quite swiftly) in front of the giant oak tree, which stood in front of the Mayor's House; that was quite grand and spacious. The 'family' started to chant and skip awkwardly around the tree. I watched in amazement as they performed their 'ritual' sort of routine. Then, they stopped and the toddler waved his hand. The tree lost all of its branches and they ran away! Then the tree trunk rose into the air, taking its roots and some of the ground with it. It transformed into a gold, jewelled door with four shapes embedded within the structure.

The family each pulled out of thin air, a Star, Diamond, Triangle and Circle amulets. One of these was blue, another pink, one emerald green and the final one amber (it reminded me of the treacle sky and the eclipse.) Then the foursome got in to a line and started to chant in some unknown and eerie language. I thought they must have been Maoris or at least supernatural beings. The unknown 'creatures' started to walk slowly to the door. The middle - aged man placed the blue star into the slot and it glowed with an almighty light. The elderly woman placed the emerald circle into her slot and it glowed with such power and courage. Then the teenage girl placed the pink diamond into the compartment and like the two before it glowed ever so brightly. Then the last amulet, which the Toddler owned, was placed into the final slot, with me transfixed in the blinding colours of the door. The door was now unlocked and slowly creaked open. The elderly woman picked me up and threw me inside! I couldn't believe it, as they followed me in and locked the door behind them...

Inside the door it was quite creative and mysterious. There were four hammocks slowly swaying in the wind. There was a large brown branch next to the battered hammocks and a rough, dinted chest between the swaying bed and the 'clothes rack.' The middle - aged man launched me across the room onto a hammock. I bent my hand back and I think I sprained my foot. While I was nursing my hand all sorts of thoughts were racing and screaming in my head:

WHAT WAS GOING TO HAPPEN TO ME?
WERE THEY GOING TO KILL ME, OR WOULD I SURVIVE?
WOULD I BECOME ONE OF THEM?

The thoughts were getting more gruesome and slightly disturbing. But the thoughts and possibilities were pushed to the back of my mind when the 'tribe' approached me. They moved slightly slowly, carrying a scroll, a bright but attractive sapphire suit, sinister looking meat and a large Technicolor amulet. This was encrusted with the four shapes that had helped unlock the doorway to hell. The man gave me the suit that strangely reminded me of the story of Joseph. He threw it at me with some force and told me to change my wardrobe. (He wrote the words down, because he knew I couldn't understand his language.) I took my Acorn High Uniform, threw it onto a nearby branch and hastily sprang into my new eerie nightmare. The elderly woman gave me the scroll, but specifically told me not to open it when I crossed the door. The teenage girl gave me the meat - like substance. She told me to eat it! I refused and refused and refused but she squeezed my nose until I couldn't obviously breath. I couldn't resist, I had to open my mouth. In my next breath I felt it in between my teeth. Surprisingly, it tasted like normal sausages at first. But, the tasty sensation soon left my mouth when a blue oozy liquid spilled out into every nook and cranny! I had no choice but to spit it out. To my surprise, the strange beings were not growling nor grunting, but smiling at me! Then the toddler crawled over the wall and sat in front of it and began moving his small hands. Words began to form themselves across the rough, cold stone wall. They read:

MY NAME IS GARINUS, MY SISTER IS AGNESCA, MY GRANDMOTHER IS NAMED RHODA AND MY FATHER IS CALLED AIDRIAN. YOU ARE PART OF OUR PROPHESY AND IT HAS NOW BEGUN.

There I was standing, thinking: Why me, why have I been chosen? I realised that my life would never be the same again and so I asked them why. The toddler wrote a series of words - courage, bravery and loyalty. I thought my brain was going to drown in all my thoughts and questions. I started to break down and I knew I was going to cry (I wasn't a softie in high school, but I wasn't particularly brave either.) But I couldn't, there was some force holding back every possible tear. A small, blue tear finally managed to squeeze its way through my eye socket. BLUE!!!!! My tears were BLUE! I thought that it was just a slight cold, but I knew it wasn't. Garnius took something out of his small, trouser pocket, a strange if plain box. It was hard wood, maybe oak. It had a medieval like quality with vines carved around the sides. The box started to glow an eerie, yet magical gold. Garnius placed his left hand in the centre. A short sound was suddenly released from the box, like a click from a computer mouse.

My mind began to wander. I started to think what my life would be like after this strange chronicle in my life had ended. While I started to leave reality and thought more about this dilemma, I came to believe that I only had a fifty-fifty chance of staying alive. Why had this happened to me out of all the kids in the world? After all, I had a pretty boring, average human life, WHY?

I was now concentrating on Garnius and the mysterious wooden box. Twenty ruby blocks emerged from inside the box. The box made a tower and then changed from ruby, emerald, topaz, aquamarine, diamond and amethyst. They reminded me of traffic lights back home, bright and British....... My attention was brought back to Garnius and his actions. He placed his soft, yet tiny hand on the top of the ruby, then the emerald block as he mumbled the word, *"Picasta..."* The blocks flew around the room and forced themselves into the crisp, rotting stone. The blocks projected words in English:

YOU HAVE ATTEMPTED TO EAT THE SACRED PUKAHAN, NOW YOU ARE HALF VAMPIRE.

BATHROOMS
As I gawped at the crescent moon above I thought about a word, just one, Vampire. I thought all of that were just stories; I and my friends loved blood and vampires, but this was just too scary and real. As I began to come back to the real world, Rhoda and Adrian took my very sore limbs and threw me into a wardrobe - like space. The door was locked behind me.......

Blue tears filled my face and made a fairly large stain on the tilting, limestone floor. Inside the room, it was dimly lit by several black candles. There was a dark, slate sink with shiny, bronze taps. There was also a giant, jagged mirror hanging on the rough wall. The majority of the room was filled with racks of metallic towels and many scented soaps. I watched my police watch slowly tick by. I was locked in the room for several hours. I soon decided after a long period of time and worry, to find a way out. It started to get colder and water started to trickle from the ceiling. There was a hole! I could finally run away from this nightmare. I moved the candles from the table, but the towels caught fire! I had to escape quickly or the eerie creature would find out that I was gone.... I grabbed the table and jammed it directly under the large hole in the ceiling. I hoisted myself up and grabbed the edge of the roof and pulled. ....

   I WAS FREE.

As I hoisted myself through the gateway to heaven, I could hear the 'bathroom' door unlocking whilst Agnesca and Rhoda cursed and blamed one another within. I jumped and landed on a pile of gravel outside the Mayor's house. The gold door was opening. Rhoda and Agnesca were quickly snapping their heads in every direction to see which way I went. Rhoda saw me and started yelling spontaneously as the four supernatural beings submerged from the door and began to chase after me.... As I began to sprint away from them, I attempted to come up with an idea for them to lose track of me... think... think! 'The Graveyard!' I ran down a public bridleway. As I stopped, I remembered this was where the local gang hung out after dark. It was now

11.47p.m., so I stopped behind a tree to listen for any noises or look for any sign of life…Light suddenly flooded into the public path. A nearby streetlamp flickered to life. I could see better, but it wasn't a great improvement. I began to run away from the foursome as they were just turning round the corner. I had another great idea swim through my mind vortex – 'Climb over the wall!' So again, I pulled myself up the extended torchlight and hoisted myself over the brown, brick wall. When I made it onto the sinking grass surface of the cemetery, without thinking, I ran and slid into a crypt! My mind and stomach were weighed down with guilt and regret. Inside the crypt was jam-packed with spiders and their 'homes.' Other parts of the ceiling were filled with mangled skeletons and corpses. Beyond the webs and worry was a passage leading somewhere into the city (I could faintly hear cars and their horns blaring), so I set off. Two, or three steps into the journey, four, muscular figures drowned the light out of the dusty and dense grave. Five, bright coloured letters came sinking into the crypt; J.O.N.A.S, they spelt my name. Before I could shout a reply, I remembered obviously that I was hiding and the letters disintegrated and disappeared like smoke. I began my voyage even more cautiously and quietly so I could hear if they entered the passage……

Along the passage there were rats, mice and spiders from species I thought never existed. About halfway down the passageways, there was a passage turning left. At the end there was a ladder with a sewage sign on its metal base. The noise of cars and taxi traffic were loud enough to confirm that I was close to the road. I went to try and see where the ladder wound up. On the wall was written in luminous, yellow marker (probably from road workers): 20-50 MacKaye Estate. That was my estate. So I climbed the ladder to the top and lifted the heavy, metal lid off the heavenly life saver and hoisted myself to safety...

GROUNDING AND DREAMING

The hole led me to a pavement just next to the gated estate that I lived in. I quickly lifted myself out of the hole and closed it behind me with my foot. I put in the security code and the black, metal gate opened slowly and I ran home and didn't stop....... When I got home I waited outside for a moment to come up with a good excuse for why I was so late. When I decided to come in, I had a negative instinct in my gut that she just knew that I was lying. (Mum is a psychologist. She is paid $1000 a day. That's why we moved, for the great opportunity, education and MONEY!)

Whilst I was pacing up and down, four hooded figures were walking in straight lines (two by two) towards my house, the people!!! I began to panic and then I knocked on the door fearing that they were going to get me. My mum answered the door and she was puffy and teary eyed up to the hills. The people were still approaching me with that slow, eerie walk. My mum started to hug me and kiss me on the forehead and then she yelled at my dad to come quick to the door. The four now formed a straight line and started to walk down my front porch. Their robes started to glow the same colour as their own amulet. My mum and dad started to quickly change their emotions to fear and woe when they recognized that there were four completely hooded strangers heading for their son. I started to walk backwards. I tripped on a lawn gnome statue and landed on my butt in the middle of my porch. I dragged myself back to the corner of my house and the gate leading to the back garden. They all finally closed in on me. My parents started to cry with fear as I asked the four creatures-

"What are you?"

They answered simply:

"Vampires. You. Sacrifice."

I started to scream. My yell was muffled with my parents and I closed my eyes and I counted down to the end of my life.........

My 'Marilyn Manson' alarm clock began to sing my favourite song, 'Putting Holes in Happiness' as I woke up and prepared for the Monday ahead. I got washed and dressed and set off on my usual route to school. (I had my breakfast on the way there, toast!) When I got to school, Beth, Lauren and Jake were at their usual spot and I walked over to them and reviewed with them what happened in Doctor Who and Eastenders at the weekend.

The bell went and we started off to our first lesson, Geography with Mrs. Mason. On the whiteboard, when she had taken the register, she wrote:

SPECIAL REPORT- ON VAMPIRES' ORIGINS

My friends and I shared confused looks to one another and then we concentrated on the lesson. I looked out of the window. There were four, hooded figures standing in the centre of the school courtyard. Had I seen them before...I wondered?

Brandon Noble

'Alnwick' by Mark Denton, 2008

Shinobi Vs Dragon Ninja

"The icy, cold winds blew towards the two paths ahead. The sign pointing which way to go had disappeared. Larry the leprechaun didn't know how to leave the castle of Olah."

Shinobi Vs Dragon Ninja

The icy, cold winds blew towards the two paths ahead. The sign pointing which way to go had disappeared. Larry the leprechaun didn't know how to leave the castle of Olah. So he had two choices: to go through the spooky forest where the crooked and magical witch, Yamz lived, or the eerie path where the troll named Gilbert lived. Larry chose the more stupid option. But what was ahead?

Larry went up the path towards the forest. Even though he was scared, he started talking to himself.

"Hello evil Larry. How are you today?"

"Hi goody two shoes Larry."

Larry soon got bored with talking to himself, so he started to sing and dance up the path. The cold, eerie winds gave him a shiver down his spine and he suddenly stopped and fell to the ground with a thud.

The evil witch, Yamz had come along on her broom. She had come back through the forest and saw the leprechaun on the floor in front of her eyes. Yamz thought she was in luck and a rainbow was nearby with a pot of gold at the end of it. Larry soon woke up and Yamz left in a puff of smoke. He thought he had been dreaming because he saw his arch nemesis Yamz towering over him. Larry carried on walking through the deepness of the forest of Olah. What lay beneath the dark, unwanted exterior of this forest?

Larry trekked through the forest alone and unwanted. If only he had a friend apart from evil Larry. This made him upset. As the sun settled in the distance, Larry set up camp for himself to sleep within for the night. There was a glimmer of light in the sky; Larry thought God had heard his cries for a friend and granted his wish to get rid of evil in the world. Then he heard a figure shouting from the distance.

"*Larry, evil hasn't left the world, you need to defeat the evil Yamz and army of evil minions if you want to restore peace to the world.*"

Larry cried back –

"*Do I have to? Surely good will conquers evil. It did in Harry Potter.*"

The voice went away and faded out into the distance. Larry was alone wondering why the voice asked him to defeat Yamz. Was it because he was Irish?

Later on throughout the forest, Larry suddenly fell to his knees, hoping that he would get a friend soon. He was tired of being alone. Then out of nowhere...

BANG!

Larry hid behind the tree stump hopefully thinking that the strange figure that didn't seem to be doing much wouldn't see him. Larry stood up and noticed the figure was an odd garden gnome, dressed with Larry's clothes from his back and a grey beard. Larry took a liking to the gnome and named it Alfie.

"*Dia duit.*" Larry spoke too soon.

"*What did you say? I don't speak that language,*" Alfie questioned.

"*I said hello, stupid,*" Larry replied.

"*I'm not going to talk to you now. You have insulted me.*"

Larry apologised for his inappropriate behaviour and slowly slumped to the ground that he wasn't far off from.

He walked away hoping Alfie would forgive him and not be a spoilsport. Alfie was new to these parts and didn't know about the culture around here.

"So where am I?"

"The city of Olah," Larry answered. *"Why do you want to know?"*

"Just wondering… Are there any good things around here like battles and duels?"

"There will be one soon between the evil Yamz and I plus her evil army of minions."

Larry told the story to Alfie of why God had told him to capture Yamz and defeat her army of minions that were actually evil skunks mesmerised by Yamz's evil powers of being good looking and smart.

"How did you get here anyway?" Larry asked. *"You just arrived out of thin air. Where did you live before you arrived in Olah?"*

"Oh right, I don't know," Alfie said slightly edgily.

Larry and Alfie walked in a dodgy line towards the dreaded house of Yamz. They knew she was hiding away from Satan, hatching a plan of world domination with her evil minion followers - skunks and hamsters. But in a flash on the other side of the forest were two superheroes, Renlik and Sehcnip with the greatest power of all: to be rock and roll heroes. They were in a band named Bleeding Heart, they had magic powers, in that they could fly, sing and play music. They were pretty good heroes, but something wasn't quite right about writing a song using what nature intended.

"How about: I went to pick you a flower, turned out it was a Venus fly trap. It bit my head so I killed it and I got you this piece of grass instead," Sehcnip suggested.

"No, *that's too lame to ever be a song,*" Renlik answered. *"But this sounds cooler: I'm secretly frying your brain cells."*

"Why didn't I think of that? That's awesome," Sehcnip replied back to Renlik.

Back to Larry and Alfie, they settled down and made camp for the night underneath the massive chestnut tree in the forest. Not long after Larry soon dropped off to sleep in the sinister forest. Alfie was relieved he had a friend like Larry. Ever since he left the back yard of his owner Knarf, he had never had a real friend. While thinking about it all, Alfie started to cry. He remembered all the good times, until his owner found a new friend called Cindups. Alfie got treated like a slave, so he waddled away. That night, Larry had a nightmare about all the bad things that happened in his life.

How sad is it that two really good friends find out about each other in the forest of Olah? There is something always popping out of the ground like mushrooms and secrets you don't want to know about. Sehcnip and Renlik, a couple of idiots but smart when they wanted to be, scored some hit records back in their day, as my mum told me. They weren't really that old, if you don't count 100 years old as ancient. But the interesting thing was that Renlik was 1 month and 12 days older than Sehcnip.

Larry and Alfie's story is totally different to that of our infamous superheroes. Little did Larry know, but Alfie had been kidnapped. Larry looked everywhere for him, but he couldn't find Alfie. Larry was alone in the forest. He shouted out loud for Alfie to come back. Larry walked through the forest alone yet again. There he was.... Alfie's body was in a pool of cider. Larry cried and mourned over his best friend's body. He tried to wake up from his nightmare but nothing happened. He was too late. Alfie was dead. Larry turned around in a sudden state of shock; there was a strange breeze that tingled across the back of his neck. He turned back around to look at Alfie's body, but it had disappeared. Larry screamed and ran away from the empty pool of apple cider.

Renlik and Sehcnip actually found Alfie's body just lying there on the floor. Sehcnip took a drink from the cider. Renlik was disgusted with Sehcnip and carried Alfie's body away from there. Later, she took his body back to base camp wrapped up in her cape. Renlik had a song from childhood to bring people back to life. Unknowingly she needed Sehcnip to help her with the song and the moves. They set up for the song with Alfie placed in the middle.

Larry heard a sweet sound coming from a hole in the tree. It made him feel all tingly inside. He followed the sound to a tree where he saw Alfie's body in the middle of the circle. The music stopped and he took a breath of fresh air. Alfie jumped into the air with joy and ran to Larry hugging him tightly.

Larry and Alfie thanked Sehcnip and Renlik with all their heart and they climbed out of the tree...There she was, Yamz and her evil minions through the forest, burning everything in sight. They drew closer towards Larry, Alfie, Renlik and Sehcnip. Alfie waddled closer to see the evil Cindups leading the way with Yamz, holding hands. The hobgoblin that had replaced him in his owner's life. The anger fired up in Alfie's eyes, steam came out of his ears. Renlik disappeared; Larry and Alfie seemed to be floating in air not long after. They were carried across the future battlefield. Larry who was carrying them across looked up in shock. He couldn't believe his eyes.

Cindups did kill his owner then went to join up with Yamz. He was the ruler of anything in darkness and evil, she was the ruler of anything that died. The minions were under her powers but in secret, they really hated her. They had nothing to break out of the spell so they just followed orders as normal. People died if they didn't follow orders while in the power of Yamz. There was always more sadness than ever when someone special had died. The Lord and ruler of the world didn't make it out alive. He had the best chance of making a team to destroy things, but even he died...his own brother. His flesh and blood had killed him. What a backstabber. It was the Lord's 120th birthday.

It had all started when Yamz met the Lord at the age of 100. It was love at first sight for the Lord. He had hearts coming out of his head. But as for Yamz she just saw the pound signs. He asked for her hand in marriage but she refused over and over again, but that night Yamz had found someone special, Eiknarf, the Lord's brother. When the Lord found out, he had suicidal thoughts towards himself. The big night was disappointing, the Lord was in his bed chamber, and he walked slowly towards the balcony, held a gun to his head and BANG!!

Blood shot and tears across the whole kingdom. Yamz and Eiknarf got married but Eiknarf had the most terrible disease, the ABC. The ABC was horrible, it made your legs go green and drop off. It had killed mostly everyone in the kingdom apart from the ones who were rich enough to have vaccines. But when everyone gave Eiknarf one year to live, it was a bit strange because he had lasted twenty years longer than his brother.

Let the battle begin!

Renlik talked to the dragon ninjas on his walkie-talkie.

"Emergency, you're needed at the battlefield!"

There were thousands of them, but Yamz had loads more. Everyone thought good would defeat evil, how would it this time? With the good side with dragon ninjas, what did Yamz have up her sleeves? Larry and Alfie called on the life stream to help them. The whole galaxy, in one place at the same time. It always helped with anything to do with good defeating evil or crushing the nightmares of Yamz achieving world domination.

Renlik began to sing as loud, as rock music ever intended her to. They sent the vampires and zombies back to sleep. Everyone was singing along with Renlik, apart from Yamz. She screamed at her minions to get back to work and kill the opposition. They were out of the spell, the music stopped and there was an awkward silence. Everyone turned to Yamz as if she was the most wanted criminal in the kingdom. She fell to her knees, begging for forgiveness, saying it wasn't her fault. Larry hobbled towards Yamz.

"Have I seen you somewhere before?" wondered Larry, as the sun's rays caught the back of his neck.

"*Of course you have. I gave you away as a child,*" answered Yamz.

"*What are you saying? That I'm your son or something else.*" Larry was confused.

"*That you are my son, Larry and your brother is…*"

Renlik ran up behind Yamz like a bolt of lightning and knocked her over.

"*Nooooo!!*" Larry shouted.

"*That was my mum, idiot!*"

Larry fell to the floor near Yamz's cold body. He burst into tears not knowing his brother was his best friend. Larry slumped all the way home, back to base camp. Renlik had fallen out with Sehcnip because she started being controlling over her. That was Renlik's story but what really happened was when the Shinobis and the Dragon Ninjas went to battle, Sehcnip had had a secret meeting with Satan over joining Yamz's gang.

"*Oh great Satan, may I ask you a favour of your worthless…I mean insane power across the galaxy?*"

"*It depends what the favour is…minion!*"

"*Minion? But Satan I need a favour from you?*"

"*From me? I'll write a letter to you. What's your address?*"

"*13 Unlucky Road, Tree Lover, T5E 7I0*"

"*Why do you need it?*"

"*I said I'm writing you a letter. Were you listening?*"

Satan rose to the challenge that Sehcnip had given him. When she took the stairway to Earth, Renlik stood there impatiently. All the way back to the tree, Renlik had ignored Sehcnip.

"*Why were you in hell?*" Renlik wondered.

"*Why should I answer to you?*" Sehcnip answered sarcastically.

"*Maybe if you told me why you were there, we wouldn't be in this mess with Yamz,*" Renlik shouted to Sehcnip.

"*We,*" Sehcnip quoted. "*This had nothing to do with you anyway.*" She looked around at the devastation that Yamz had caused and her minions had worsened.

As Larry walked onto the battlefield it was not just to see his best friend there, crouching over Yamz's body. Larry wondered why Yamz had had such a big impact on Alfie's life.

"*Why does Yamz have such an impact on your life?*" Larry asked.

"*Here, she would like for you to see this.*" Alfie passed a screwed up picture of Yamz, to Larry.

"*Why are you on this, Alfie?*"

"Because, I'm your brother," Alfie replied.

Larry told Alfie what happened on the battlefield. A strange fog gathered across the land. What lay beneath it?

Amy Kilner

An extract from the novel – 'Laughter in light and darkness'

CHAPTER 1- ALIVE

Annabella walked into school as usual. It was around quarter past eight, meaning she had fifteen minutes left until the bell went signalling the beginning of Wednesday's lessons (which wasn't bad timing by Annabella's standards at all.) The sun was shining through the thin layer of clouds and patches of calm sea blue were dotted around, for the small Yorkshire village today was a very pleasant day indeed. It was spring now in England and cherry blossoms flowered on nearby trees. Annabella loved cherry blossoms, but not even that could lift the dark mood she was in now...

The morning so far had been pretty average, she had woken up at seven am and let out the biggest groan she could muster because she despised getting up early. She had gone and put on her school's black summer shirt and her trousers, then looked at herself in the mirror. She had blonde hair that went just past her shoulders and grew at an alarming rate, blue eyes that didn't even have a glimmer of brown in them like some people had, but the thing that made her look so different was the sheer paleness of her skin, like new fallen snow, that seemed to highlight her dark pink lips. In Goldfield many people were pale, however, their paleness just made them look a light yellow. Not like Annabella.

She had set off for school as usual. It was only about a mile, probably less because she could walk it in twenty minutes to half an hour. Annabella didn't mind walking anymore. In winter she had walked in the frosty, chilling morning where she could see her own breath and she had often got her dad to drop her off instead, but even that had its drawbacks, as she sat with her teeth chattering in the defrosting car. Still, Annabella preferred winter. Cold wasn't the worse thing in the world, in fact, she liked snow better than sun. Snow can make you feel clean and fresh, whereas sun makes you feel greasy and clammy (although walking a mile in the snow is still a daunting prospect for a twelve - year - old little girl). Nah, the thing that put her in a bad mood today was something she couldn't put her finger on... she felt deep down something was wrong and her feelings were usually right...

Her best friends were gathered near the school gates again today. It had become the normal meeting place lately because their last place had been taken over by a new group. That was how it worked, when little children play forts, pretending to defend their bases, they didn't realise they were actually practising for the real thing in high school. But it's not quite the same, unless of course you have a catapult handy and some armour stuffed in your school bag. She sped up to meet them, pouncing on Joan playfully and she pretended to jump and they collapsed into fits of laughter. They were probably the most random kids in the school after all, so she had to make an entrance. Annabella ceased giggling and joined the others in the cluster.

Her closest friends were all there. The group consisted of three boys and three girls including her; Lukas, Michael and Ted were the males (if you could call them that) and Joan, Rosie and herself were the girls. In Annabella's opinion, they were the closest any children could get; they all had age ranges of eleven to twelve and some had gone to primary together (Annabella had gone to Lacely with Ted and Lukas), but none of that really mattered. Those six would end up together no matter what...

"*EMO,*" yelled a ginger-haired boy from across the playground. "*Scum!*" The group ignored it as if they couldn't hear. One of the things they had in common was that they were bullied; because of course they were different...

Every day they let themselves be pushed around and called names. At first, it had bothered them, especially Joan and Annabella who had it worse than the others, but now they had let it kill them so many times it didn't hurt them anymore.

"*Rosie?*" asked Annabella, taking her attention away from the gathering bullies; she didn't want them to be scared. "*Please tell me we don't have history first...*" Rosie grinned and told her they had and there was a rather dramatic collective groan. It was a sort of running joke amongst them - their history teacher was the kind that actually made them think of jumping from the three storey high window and taking their chances...

"*You'd think she would have been charged for torture by now,*" Ted grinned. Lukas and Joan giggled and started doing impressions of different teachers while Annabella looked around nervously at the bullies.

They chatted as usual for a while about boys and English and Ted started reminiscing about old times as if he were around eighty. Rosie started to play truths with Lukas, which seemed to be going well...

Annabella decided it was time they moved so she walked with the girls over to the road and waited to cross. An old Civic sped down the road and they waited for it to pass so they could cross to the benches by the technology block. Suddenly however, Annabella felt a hard force push her into the road a moment before the Civic went past and she fell into the road and sprawled across the floor. On impact, she automatically tensed, expecting, almost hoping that the car would hit her. Fortunately, it didn't... The car had managed to slam its brakes on a second before it got to her. She didn't feel relief at this however; just blind fury at the person who had pushed her. She picked herself up, not honestly caring if she had broken anything and turned to glare at her attacker. When she saw him she felt more anger surging through her veins. He wasn't even looking at her now; his focus was on Rosie who he was now advancing on. Annabella was filled with rage, she didn't give a damn if he hurt her, but if he touched Rosie she would kill him.

Rosie backed off, her eyes hiding her fear while trained on the long jagged stick he had in his hand. Annabella surged towards him using all the fire that had been doused and she had just rekindled... She grabbed him by the shoulder and spun him round; he hadn't expected it and lost grip on his mundane weapon as she punched him hard in the face. A crowd of teens were gathering around her now, as they always did when there was going to be a fight. The crowd somehow made a perfect circle around them as the boy got back up. He grinned stupidly and launched at Annabella, grabbing her arm and pushing her back into the fence. He pinned her there and kicked her in the stomach, but she barely felt it now and neither could she hear the noise of the crowd...All she could feel was the rhythm of her heart in her ears. Her heart however didn't beat with fear or anxiety...it was beating with excitement...

Annabella head-butted the boy hard and he stumbled back. She wasted no time on grabbing him. She hit him as many times as she could in a minute, that deadly rhythm blocking out reality leaving only this wonderful feeling of being alive. He grabbed her hair with a brute force and pulled her away hitting her hard in the face, temporarily making her vision cloud. She was beginning to feel the pain in her head now and she flailed out desperately trying to push him off, letting her instincts take over her body. She grabbed his throat then and she irrevocably lost it. Annabella squeezed his neck, digging her nails into his throat, not really making the decision to kill him but not really caring. Blood began to spill over her hands as the boy kicked and pulled in her arms while staring into her eyes, mesmerised by the change in the way she looked. Before, her eyes had seemed so hollow and resigned, almost dead... but now her eyes were filled with a roaring fire of hate and anger. It almost looked like she could unleash hell with a blink...

The blood was everywhere now; it ran over her hands and down her uniform, making the smell of rust and salt cloud her nose. The teachers who had been trying to push through since the crowd had begun to gather finally managed to get through and Annabella felt rough hands pull her back from the boy who fainted a moment later. One teacher screamed as she saw all the blood. Annabella didn't care anymore. She shrugged off the teachers and walked to where they were taking her, ignoring their cautious glances at each other. For a minute at least, Annabella was happy. For the first time in months, Annabella felt alive again

'Remove' was the centre of Annabella's school; it served many purposes. For one, it was where people who were getting bullied went so that the bullies could be shouted at (like that ever did anything.) However, the main reason 'Remove' was there was to deal with fights and school crimes, but somehow Annabella doubted anybody had been brought here for strangling someone. Then again, Annabella thought, this was her school. No one had shouted at her yet, which worried Annabella. If you had ever done something really serious, the only thing worse than being told off was not getting told off, because that meant they were still so shocked they weren't sure what to do...She knew the police had been called and an ambulance had already taken the boy away, so all she could do was wait for the inevitable.

The teachers had been unable to contact her mum, but they'd left a message so it wouldn't be long before her mother would be calling. Annabella couldn't be sure what her mum would say. Her mum had always defended her and helped her, but then again she'd never almost killed anyone...

She sat on the edge of the old blue sofa in 'Remove' for a moment, deep in thought. She knew she was falling again, she could feel it. After a minute or two, she gathered her knees to her chest and stared at her jeans in the darkness she'd made by blocking out the light with her arms. Now Annabella didn't have to fight back the tears, once again Annabella felt nothing...

Various people walked in an out throughout the time Annabella sat there. She felt their eyes linger on her with curious looks and some muttered nonchalantly about her and what had happened earlier. After she had been sitting there for about twenty minutes, a girl from her class came in to get a dress code with what seemed to be her friend and Annabella distinctly remembered hearing the words *'crazy'* and *'dangerous'* in a hushed conversation between the kids. She smirked to herself, half tempted to jump up and really give the girls something to talk about. However seeing the girls together, so happy and carefree made her want to be with her friends back in English or Maths, laughing and swapping sweets under the table. She sighed inwardly - what would her friends think of her now? They might hate her too, she'd made herself look crazy and dangerous... but then again she had only been protecting them... she had always protected them.

Annabella didn't want her friends to end up like her. When you're depressed or empty people think you want to know there are others like you, but in Annabella's case she was relieved no one felt like she did, especially not her friends. No child should feel like her, no one at all should feel like she did, but she knew that if she wasn't there to protect her friends, shield them from the world, then they would end up empty too ...Annabella knew they had no idea what it was like inside her head. She smiled. She acted as though she was happy and bright because she didn't want anyone to try and save her. Annabella didn't need saving, Annabella could save herself...She guarded the water with fire...

Annabella thought about all the people who had seen her attack, until her mind rested on Josh. Josh didn't pick on Annabella but he did annoy her. It wasn't that he pestered her, but the fact he was so smart and had the ability to become so much more, yet he squandered it. Most people would have seen Josh as just another annoying teenager with no empathy or second thought on what they do, but Josh did. Annabella could see it in his eyes, the way he looked, the way he seemed to see her... not to the full extent, but fairly clearly compared to the boys he befriended. He had begun to have second thoughts on her strength after she hadn't reacted to anyone for a while. She smiled cruelly and wondered what he thought now.

There was a knock at the 'Remove' door. Annabella ignored it and kept flicking through the magazine she had picked up off the side table, an old issue of Kerrang. Annabella had read it already but she decided she needed something to distract her from the current situation she was in. Miss Reeds opened the door and talked to the person outside the door. Annabella heard her say 'dear' so it wasn't the police at least. The voice through the door was unusually silky and cool; the accent definitely wasn't from around here and was all masculine. Curious, Annabella looked up from her magazine to see two males enter the room. One looked around twenty-five and the other looked about her age, possibly a little older...She observed their appearance particularly carefully; the older man had long brown hair that seemed to lighten at the tips and end in blonde, he had blue eyes like hers, except his seemed like crystal, un-flawed and beautiful, they almost looked like they had been crafted by a great artist. He wore a black shirt with the cuffs opened slightly and some matching trousers that suited his figure and made him look even more muscular. The boy didn't take away from his handsomeness either. The kid, like him had sparkling blue eyes, but instead of brown hair he had black hair that reached just past his ears and framed his undoubtedly male face. The boy wore a similar outfit to what Annabella presumed was his father except his shirt was white and opened slightly at the top. She stared at them for a moment without real-izing, more or less analyzing them.

Annabella began to use the art she had learnt since she came to high school. She began to try and see if they were a threat or not. In order to survive in a place like that, you needed to know whom you could trust and who to avoid. She looked at them as they talked to the teacher, their lips curving into a smile now and again, when the taller man turned and looked at her directly in the eyes. Annabella had the urge to look at the floor as most people did around there, but she didn't. She was sick of doing what everyone else did. She wasn't everyone else! And she wanted them to know it!

They maintained eye contact for what seemed a long time. He seemed to dig into her eyes as if searching for something, but he didn't seem unfriendly. After a while, he smiled and turned to the teacher who looked a little worried now; he approached Annabella slowly.

"*Laklin,*" he said smiling.

Annabella looked back at him, probably showing her confusion.

"*Annabella,*" she replied.

"*Now what's a nice girl like you doing in a place like this looking so...miserable?*" She didn't see any point in lying to him.

"*How would you know if I was nice? You can't allow appearances to fool you, but I don't blame you, I even fooled myself into thinking I was nice. I am here because I just tried to kill someone. Does that answer your question?*" She knew she had made herself sound like a psychopath but she didn't care. Laklin didn't look shocked as she had expected, but he did look at her with an odd yet unreadable expression.

"*You are a nice girl,*" he said, with an annoyed tone touching the edges of his voice, "*and you're also strong. What you do to survive is your business and you shouldn't be mocked for it.*"

Annabella couldn't believe his insight; how would he know about survival? Adults didn't think like that, they didn't understand the way the world works. Annabella suddenly became aware of everyone in the room staring at her like she was some sort of freak show and Laklin stood up and walked back over to Miss, smiling again as if nothing had happened.

"*So Drakus will be attending this school on Monday?*" Laklin asked.

"*Yes,*" said Miss, regaining her composure. "*All that is left to do is to sort out the matter of sets and forms now. In my previous talks with Drakus, I think he'd be perfectly fine in all top sets, but who do you recommend as his guardian?*" Annabella noted she said guardian.

"I think he'll be perfectly fine in top sets," said Laklin, casually glancing at Drakus and smiling.

"Good," said Miss. *"Now as for forms, in Year Seven, you have a choice."* She passed a sheet of paper to Drakus and he looked at it for only a second, then looked at Annabella for the first time since he'd entered the room.

"What form is she in?" he asked the teacher. She looked flustered and went over to a computer, probably pulling up Annabella's profile from the school's mainframe.

"Annabella is in 7LT," she said. Annabella wondered for a moment why she wasn't just asked.

"Then that's the form I want to be in," said Drakus.

CHAPTER 2- ANGER

Annabella ran out onto the football pitch for PE with Rosie and Joan, her mood was light and they were all laughing and smiling happily at each other. The police had come, but it was easy for Annabella to explain herself out of trouble. She told them it had been self-defence, which it had, sort of... She told them about the bullying and how he had attacked her and her friends. They were surprisingly nice about the whole thing and the school said they would suspend the boy who had fought Annabella. Her mum had reacted really well and told her she had done right by defending herself and her friends. She didn't tell them about the feeling alive bit of course, she didn't need an asylum visit right now. The usual bullies still picked on them, but they were a little more careful about what they did to Annabella's friends. She hadn't expected them to treat her differently after she had publicly admitted to it being a complete accident and she hadn't meant to grab his throat (they were idiots after all so it wasn't shocking they believed her.)

The only thing that was annoying Annabella at that moment was that it was Monday and she still hadn't seen Drakus. Had he changed his mind and gone to another school? It wouldn't have surprised her, considering the performance on Wednesday, but she had to admit she had been looking forward to getting to know the mysterious boy who had taken such an interest in her. She tore down the field putting Drakus to the back of her mind, there was no point thinking about a boy she had just met when she had so many other problems...

They had a supply teacher that day, which really didn't affect Annabella's situation. Her regular teacher was just as useless when it came to tackling the girls in her class. They had just started their rounders unit and Joan, Rosie and her, all picked up a bat and joined the queue, ignoring the whispers behind them. Rosie was the first up of the three of them and they wished her luck as she stepped up. Rosie hit it fairly hard for her then ran to first base making it just in time. Joan stepped up and missed it completely the first time and then hit it the second. Annabella stepped up and winked at Joan who was at first base. They had a plan to get them both out quickly since they both hated P.E. Annabella stepped up and Jane took the bowl. She threw it hard but evenly and she managed to hit it with the side of the bat and then ran. When she started to run so did Joan who then stopped at the second, but Annabella kept going and ran Joan out. They grinned at each other as they walked off and the other team cheered at already getting two players out.

Rosie rolled her eyes at them and smiled mouthing she wanted to stay in and Annabella grinned and wished her luck.

After a while Joan and Annabella started talking amongst themselves about little trivial things like lunch plans and where they were going on their holidays. The sun had gone behind the clouds, which were a dark grey and they guessed it would rain soon. They began to talk about bikes and Ted when, all of a sudden, Rosie darted off the field and ran, tears visibly running down her cheeks. Annabella and Joan looked at each other for a moment and then almost simultaneously looked at where Rosie had been standing. Sure enough, there was Helen Myers, one of the meanest girls in year seven. She was grinning to herself...

It only took Annabella seconds to run after Rosie and Joan soon ran after her. Rosie had managed to get all the way to the other side of the field and was sitting down now with her knees up to her chest sobbing. Annabella didn't feel the anger yet, she was too concerned for her friend, but she knew she would get Helen for this. They reached Rosie and Joan and immediately started asking her what was wrong and tried to reassure her, but Rosie said nothing and continued to cry. Annabella simply bent down and hugged Rosie tightly.

After a while Annabella released her.

"*What happened?*"

Rosie explained how Helen and Diane had threatened to beat her up at lunch and had called her some very vulgar and cruel names. Annabella fumed inside now, but it wasn't like Wednesday; she could control herself. Annabella and Joan comforted Rosie and told her it was okay for a while until she stopped crying and then stayed and chatted with her for a little while. Annabella hated thinking of her friends as weak, because they were not. They were perfectly ordinary young girls, and it was Annabella that was the weird one. Annabella was the one who needed to change, but she had to admit she wouldn't cry when Helen had said that, not on the outside anyway...

After a while the substitute began to walk over the field, her wrinkled face contorted into a red mask of bitter ugliness and a sort of fleeting pointless anger that would only lead her prune like features to become even more unattractive as she came closer. Annabella knew the teacher was going to shout at them, i.e., Joan and her and she didn't honestly care about that. When Joan and her had come over they knew what they had risked as the teacher had told them they couldn't go, but if she made Rosie any more upset than she was, she was going to be fuming...

"HOW DARE YOU!" the teacher shouted at Joan as she finally managed to waddle over. "YOU BOTH HAVE A TWENTY MINUTE DETENTION! DO YOU UNDERSTAND?"

"But...but," Joan argued feebly but the supply wasn't listening anymore.

"DO YOU UNDERSTAND?" she screamed at Annabella, who managed to nod and control her urge to yell at the horrendous excuse of a staff member and tell her exactly what she thought of her teaching skills.

Then the supply did something that was enough to infuriate Annabella's temper to the point of exhaustion:

"AND YOU," she said turning on Rosie, *"STOP BEING SUCH A LITTLE CRY BABY OVER A FEW NAMES! GET BACK OVER THERE AND APOLO-GISE!"* Rosie didn't even raise her head to this and neither should she. The stupid woman had no idea what those girls had said, had no idea about the threats and sneers and the life of a girl like Rosie! She was probably one of the girls who would have bullied them anyway! The supply continued to shout at Rosie who was now a crying wreck as the teacher called her pathetic and Joan looked at Annabella with eyes that begged her to do something. Annabella snapped:

"SHUT UP!" she yelled. *"IF YOU DID YOUR JOB PROPERLY, WE WOULDN'T HAVE TO DISOBEY YOU!"*

"DON'T YOU SPEAK TO ME LIKE THAT YOU INSOLA…"

"DON'T YOU UPSET MY FRIENDS!" Annabella shouted back even louder. *"I don't have to listen to you! You can go back to the others and pretend they are nice and you are a great teacher but we live in the real world and in the real world you stink so get lost!"* The teacher looked angry now and she shouted back –

"You stupid little child! Don't you talk to me like that! I am a teacher!"

"I don't give a stuff, ignoring people like you is what I do," she yelled and then she felt what she had been dreading, as the teacher continuously shouted at her, fire once again lit and filled her eyes. To a passerby, it would have seemed like Annabella's eyes were filled with a flame that could have devoured all in its path.

"Now you listen to me," Annabella snarled glaring at the teacher. *"You came here today thinking you would be*

baby sitting and you probably didn't think you'd have to deal with a bunch of teens picking on one kid and you know what I don't think you care. You thought you would come here and get some easy money, whether you helped any children or not. So you know what? We will help ourselves and you will go do what you think your job is and leave us alone, got it?" Annabella's eyes continued to burn while boring into the teacher's eyes, daring her to argue. Fortunately for them all, the teacher took the advice and turned around and went back to the others, trying to maintain the little dignity she had left as Annabella's fire receded.

Annabella looked back at her friends who for a moment were staring at her in awe. There was an awkward silence until Joan, obviously trying to take away the mood, said –

"That was so… awesome!" she smiled. *"Do it again."* The balance was restored. They walked back to the changing rooms. Rosie had her confidence back now and wasn't as scared when she walked in, though she did edge beside Annabella and Joan when they went passed Helen. Helen did try to say something to Rosie but Annabella blocked her way and glared at her, the fire burning in her eyes just for Helen now. When Helen backed off slightly, Annabella gave her a hand sign that summed up what Annabella thought of her completely.

They got back into their uniforms quickly and as soon as the bell went for lunch they left, making their dinner plans quickly when they met up with the boys.

"But I want to go get a sausage roll from Cooplands!" whined Lukas.

"But I need choc nibs!" stated Joan.

Annabella smiled as they argued happily over chips and chocolate and whether Andy's news was better than Paul's news or not. It was all so childish but even Annabella needed to be a child sometimes.

"So where do you want to go Annabella?" asked their other friend Heather.

"Ummm... I think I'll stay in today guys," Annabella shrugged. *"I'm not all that hungry."* The group argued with her, but Annabella stayed firm and they finally agreed to go without her and after waving goodbye the five disappeared out of the gates, walking up to their local high street in Goldfield and Heather then split with Lukas to go down to the neighbouring village.

Annabella really wasn't hungry, but the reason she wanted to stay back was because she needed some time alone, sometimes you have to be on your own for a while; it's a fact of life, especially for almost teen girls. She decided it might be nice to have a walk by herself so she took a shortcut through the back of the school field and into a small wood until she got to a quieter field. She sat down and dug her hand into her rucksack, searching for her phone. Annabella pulled it out and immediately turned 'Moonlight' by Beethoven on and then she grabbed her sketchbook and a pencil. She listened to the sonata peacefully while drawing a scene out of one of her stories. Annabella loved to write, she wrote fantasy horror stories, writing made her feel free and when she wasn't writing she was drawing scenes from her stories. She loved to write vampire stories especially...

After Moonlight ended Annabella reached over to change the song when someone spoke behind her.

"You like Beethoven?" She whipped around to see Drakus standing behind her smirking.

"Don't scare me like that!" she blushed, what was he doing here? *"Yes, I do."*

"Sorry," he smiled, making Annabella blush even more, *"I just thought it was unusual for someone your age to appreciate a sonata like moonlight."*

"Well we aren't all idiots," not trying to put so much venom into her words. *"So why are you here?"* she asked rolling her eyes.

"Oh, you know, I just thought I'd go for a walk," he grinned. *"It's a lovely day,"* he gestured to the dark building clouds.

"Oh don't give me that bull," she said.

"You've got quite a little mouth haven't you?" he said meaningfully, as if he were trying to tell her something. *"What do you want me to say, I followed you here?"* Yet again she turned red and he laughed. *"So why weren't you at school?"* Annabella did try to not sound pouty.

"Why, did you miss me?" He laughed.

"Haven't you ever skipped school before?"

"No! I was just wondering why, I didn't care or anything!" Annabella regretted saying the last bit because it made it sound a lot like she did care a hell of a lot and was trying to hide it from him.

"So," he changed the subject, *"What are you drawing?"* Annabella grabbed her sketch pad and shoved it underneath her bag.

"Nothing," she said.

"Come on, show me," he said tackling her and taking the sketchbook. Annabella tried to get it back off him, but eventually just gave up and waited to see what he thought. Annabella grew worried, with each picture his frown

deepened and then he just tossed the book on the floor. Annabella opened her mouth to say something but couldn't. Were her drawings really that bad? Drakus seemed to be gritting his teeth when he suddenly burst out with –

"Why are they all vampires?"

She frowned –

"I don't know, I've always loved drawing and writing about vampires…"

"Well stop it!" he shouted. *"Vampires aren't real!"* She frowned, why was he getting so upset over this? She decided not to argue with him and packed her things back into her bag.

"Goodbye then," she said finally. *"Will I see you tomorrow?"* She hoped the answer was yes.

"Sure," he grinned. *"Bye then and I'm sorry for snapping."* He was such a charmer.

It wasn't until English on Tuesday that Annabella next saw Drakus. Annabella had already grown bored with the low level of work in the five minutes she had been sitting there, so to distract herself, Joan and her were playing rock, paper scissors under the table. The woman running the lesson wasn't exactly their supply and wasn't exactly their real teacher either. Their teacher had got ill in the first few weeks her class had been in year seven, so they had been between substitutes for some time now. Annabella loved English, to her it opened up a whole new world where she could do what she liked when she liked – there were no boundaries for what you could think of. The class were now involved in some alliteration practice, which Annabella ignored completely and kept writing the story she was doing for her other English teacher. Like most of Annabella's stories it was about vampires.

Annabella couldn't help but be drawn to vampires, a lot of people were, but with Annabella it was as though vampires were the only people that understood her. Annabella knew they weren't real, but the elegance of them, the grace and the intelligence had become a sort of strange role model for her and sometimes the stories she imagined were the only things that stopped her falling into an abyss of nothingness. She had been writing for about ten minutes when there was a knock on the class-room door; no one looked up. It was common for teachers and students to come in and out of different classes giving messages to the staff in charge. Devon opened the door casually then sat down without saying anything, as Miss Jenkins from 'Remove' came in.

"Good afternoon class," said Miss in her Scottish accent. *"Sorry to disturb you while you seem to be working so hard, but we have a new boy today."*

Everyone stared at Drakus, especially the girls.

"This is Drakus," finished Miss Jenkins.

Miss gestured for him to take a seat somewhere and all around girls made spaces for him. Who wouldn't want to sit next to the hot, new boy? To the girls' dismay he chose to sit next to the girl they all hated, the weird one, the one they picked on, Annabella.

"Hello again, Annabella," said Drakus, making sure she was the only one that could see him smirk when everyone in the class jaws dropped.

"Hey, Drakus," she replied, smiling.

Miss Jenkins left and their teacher tried unsuccessfully to pull the class's attention back to her. Everyone wanted to know how Annabella, the Emo, knew Drakus. After Annabella had said her pleasantries, she turned her attention back to her story, ignoring the class stares. There was an awkward silence until George Cliff yelled:

"Hey Drake! Don't sit with freak you'll get lurgies!"
Drake glared at the boy –

"Picking on a girl? You're the freak." George stood up.

"What you say to me?" Drakus stood up too.

"You heard me, kid."

George walked over to Drakus and swore at him, making false threats and trying to make himself look tougher than he really was, while the poor teacher tried to get them to quieten down. Annabella stood too now, trying to calm the boys into their seats; she didn't want one of her bullies and the boy who probably thought her insane to fight.

"Stop it," she said quietly, looking at the boys, but they continued to glare at each other until George started to grin stupidly. Then, without warning, George punched her hard in the face, catching her nose and laughing as she let out a cry of pain. Annabella grabbed her face as tears started to build up from the impact. She heard something hit the ground and heard a low growl. Annabella moved her hands to see George on the floor, his eyes dazed from what must have been a punch. The class looked stunned and she turned to look at Drakus who had his back to the class so the only person who could see him was her. What she saw was horrifying... Drakus seemed to have completely changed yet stayed the same. His blue eyes had turned a black that seemed to absorb all light around them. His skin was paler now too, but the most frightening thing of all was that he had a shiny set of fangs. Drakus must have realised Annabella was looking at him, because his mouth opened and he

turned to look at her, making sure no one else could see him and his eyes turned back to blue. Annabella stood shock still, her mind in a whirl.

"*Annabella...,*" said Drakus, breathlessly, but Annabella couldn't even breath from the fear. Annabella turned and looked at the class who were all staring at her. She ran...tore down the hallway and out of the first exit door she could find into the playground. She made it to the field before she stopped running. A second later Drakus appeared at her side. She screamed and pushed him back. He grabbed her wrist and stared into her eyes.

"*Annabella! Annabella! Calm down!*" he shushed her.

"*Let go of me, vampire!*" she yelled in panic.

"*Annabella, calm down! Listen to me! Don't be scared I won't hurt you, I promise,*" he said in desperation. "*Remember those vampires in your stories? I'm just like them, Annabella. Please don't panic!*"

"I'm sick of this! You're just messing with my head! I'm sick of imagining vampires everywhere! Sick of the bullies and the lies! Leave me alone! I don't give a damn what you are!" She was in tears by now.

"*Please let me explain,*" he begged but Annabella wouldn't listen. She was scared and tired and miserable. She gave him one last fleeting look then ran home, sobbing desperately.

Annabella couldn't take it anymore. She was sick of the bullies and the brooding and that horrible feeling of being trapped somewhere she hated. Her mum worked until six pm usually and her dad until seven so she had plenty of time to pack her bags; she was running away. Annabella packed some jeans and a few t-shirts and a jacket too. She shoved some underwear in and some pyjamas. Then she went over to her skull moneybox that she had got for Christmas and took out two hundred pounds that she'd been saving up since her birthday. She put her stuff in her bag and then sat at the kitchen table and began to write a note. She read it back when she had finished:

Dear Mum, Dad and everyone else,

I love you and I always will, but I have to leave. I have spent so long worrying about making other people happy, about what others would think, but now I have to worry about myself. I'm keeping this letter short for both our sakes.
All my love,

Annabella
xxx

Annabella thought she would cry as she read the note, but she didn't... She thought she would cry when she stuck the note to the side and then walked out the front door, her rucksack on her back, but still she didn't. Annabella sighed and then thought about where she could go, it would have to be far away from here or someone would find her... She walked to the bus stop just outside The Angel pub and read the times; a bus would be here at half past. She checked her watch, only ten minutes, and then she would be gone. Gone forever...

The bus came and she got on and gave the bus driver a five-pound note and told him just to take her as far as he could. He looked at her questioningly so she slipped him another ten and he didn't ask any more questions. The bus went all the way to Huddersfield then she got off on the high street and walked along it slowly, kicking a stone, deep in thought. She came across a hotel after about half an hour, it was old and rundown with only a few stay rooms, but it would do and it only cost twenty pounds a night, she didn't expect to stay long.

The woman at the desk didn't ask anything once she'd paid. She had a thick Russian accent and a name that was so long it didn't fit on her name tag so Annabella just said her pleasantries then disappeared up to her room. The rooms weren't as bad as Annabella had thought they would be. There was a double bed, a clock, a lamp and even a TV with a coin slot to make it run. All in all it wasn't a bad place. She had only seen two other guests so far, one was a pretty young woman who always seemed to have a lollipop in her mouth and the other a strange old man that muttered to himself and dribbled a lot. They were quiet so Annabella got all the peace she needed to think. Pretty soon people would be looking for her, but she doubted they would look here. What if she was in the paper, or on the news? She couldn't stay here forever and once she went into normal civilization someone would spot her for sure. She lay on her bed and thought about how awful the week had been…and that was another thing altogether, would Drakus or Laklin look out for her? If Drakus really were a vampire he wouldn't want his secret exposing… The whole day was making her weary now, her eyelids begun to droop and she couldn't fight it anymore, sleep claimed the tired child and robbed her of her worries, at least until sunrise…

The next day Annabella awoke to the sun shining through the window of her hotel room and a new idea had hit her. She couldn't leave there and she needed money so she would apply for a job there instead... She didn't have a national insurance number, but she doubted the money grubbing owner of the hotel would care if she was cheap labour and she would dye her hair so none of the guests would recognize her. She had the whole plan worked out in her head, now all she had to do was convince the Russian woman to let her work there for her. She shoved on some of the clothes from her rucksack and bolted for the stairs to the front desk. The woman was sat there as usual and looked at her expectantly when she burst into the room out of breath.

"Yes?" asked the woman; her accent seemed different. *"How can I help you, little girl?"*

"I was wondering if...," she breathed, *"I could apply for a job here."* The woman laughed deeply.

"You have to be joking! You're what... thirteen?"

"I'm twelve, but please listen; I need a job. I come cheap and all I want is to be able to stay here, please!"

The woman watched her for a moment.

"Where are your parents?" The accent had completely disappeared now, making Annabella sure it was feigned.

"My parents are at home, I think."

"Then why do you need a job?" the woman asked.

"Because... because I ran away... and I need a job." Annabella answered relieved that the woman didn't show any sympathy; she hated people feeling sorry for her.

"I suppose I could let you work here, but it won't be easy for you, I'm not running a playhouse and if you get caught I knew nothing about you. Okay?" As the woman

said this, a feeling of lightness passed over Annabella. She had a job and she was going to be okay. Annabella nodded eagerly and listened as the woman told her the details and a few other things concerning personal matters.

Annabella had been right about the fake accent. The woman at the desk was called Alexis and she came from Scotland, but had lived most of her life in a secluded valley in Lancashire. She was a pretty woman with flame red hair and green eyes and a perfectly formed body. She only looked around twenty-two, her attitude was probably the thing that let her down the most. She talked with so much venom she could melt your face if you were the unconfident type and she loved money more than anything. Also, by the way men seemed to visit regularly and only stay a few hours 'talking' to Alexis, she thought that the woman probably found other alternative methods of making money for herself.

Annabella didn't find the job too hard really, all she did was dust and mop and make and change the beds. Annabella had also started making breakfasts for the guests if they paid for it in advance, which wasn't hard once she'd learnt to use the fryer. She didn't sleep in the guest room anymore, for obvious reasons. She slept in the staff quarters, which other than for her and Alexis was empty. They weren't great, but they were okay once she'd dusted it off and brought a spare lamp in for light, so she could read at night.

So much had changed during the now three weeks Annabella had been working at the hotel. Annabella had dyed her beautiful golden blonde hair black, which she had to admit she liked. Her pale skin and black hair made her look very gaunt, which was the way she liked it - at her old home she had always looked so full of life, but now no one would recognize her - she loved the freedom. Annabella didn't miss her old life. She had been miserable and lonely, but even so she kept thinking of how her friends and family were doing. She had been right about the news thing – she was all over the front pages of the South Yorkshire Times and she had been on Look North a week ago. Alexis never got the newspaper though and she couldn't stand TV so she didn't have to worry about her, but she kept herself scarce around customers and Alexis' clients. However one thing that didn't change was Annabella's sleeping patterns. She still had to stay up until she was dying for sleep or she would have night-mares. Annabella hated her nightmares so she had to make sure she was too tired to dream... Annabella wasn't sure if she was happy, but at least now she was free.

Bethany Pickering

The Alleyway

It was a dark, cold, terrifying night. Thunder cracked through the air like an almighty powerful whip creating an all-powerful clatter through the otherwise silent street. Rain capped the streets restricting vision and a tremendous cold passed through the air leaving anyone unfortunate enough to be outdoors with a chill that ran down their spines. The alleyways throughout were like torrential showers as the water dripped from the overhanging gutters and an almost song like noise accompanied the sounds, as cats called out to their owners to let them in. I was completely alone, as I filed down the street; this was what scared me most. I had never before seen the street in such a frightening light. I quickened my pace and my heart started racing as I worried about anything that could happen, but whatever I thought nothing prepared me for what happened next. 'Creak.' I suddenly stopped dead in my tracks as though I was glued to the spot. However scared I knew I was, I could not stand and do nothing. My heart had seemed to jump into my throat as though trying to escape my body. I turned my head cautiously to where the noise had been created. When I reached my destination I was sickened and more frightened than I'd ever been before. Stood there staring back at me was a tall, dark figure, his face blanketed by a blanket of shadow as he stood sandwiched between the figures of two thick silhouettes of houses.

Usually if this happened I would think nothing of it. Just teenagers larking around, but something about the figure's appearance startled the life out of me. The figure stood there as still as a carving, legs spread approximately two centimetres apart not moving an absolute inch. His knee-high boots were tied exactly symmetrical to one another and neatly polished, shiny black, enough to reflect the marvellous glow of the moon. His trousers were black cotton covered in many, many pockets fastened together with what looked like teeth. They were razor sharp with a dazzling white tinge. Centred almost above the furthest pocket was something that didn't affect me as for a moment I was blissfully unaware of what it could be. My legs moved closer, inch-by-inch to the scary figure as though under a spell.

I willed myself to stop, but it was no good, every speck of my body was set on a specific destination and wouldn't stop until I was there. Now as I was gradually being lugged towards the terrifying figure and the empty darkness, I could see what the thing was. It was a key, riding blissfully on the figure's dark belt. The dark skeletal key hung long. It was like nothing I'd ever seen before. As a matter of fact it was out of this world. The key shape was what I could only imagine as some kind of portal and the eyes hung in its head, red glowing, cutting through the air and the gloom of the night. I stopped suddenly with a violent jerk just one thankful metre from the now ever so looming silhouette. I prayed for that to be it. I prayed this was a ghastly dream and any moment now I would wake up and be at home in my bed, in an horrendous pool of sweat. But I was so far from the truth. Now as I stood praying I was oblivious to the fact that the figure initiated into a movement towards me. His cold hard stare held me in place as though being frozen in a tub of liquid nitrogen. The effects were instant and my muscles felt tense. I tried diligently, but whatever I seemed to do was thwarted by the cold, menacing stare, of the evil figure. The frame of the silhouette drew ever closer and I could see the ever so faint feature of his face, but what drew my attention were the figure's eyes. Alight with fire, as angry as a bull, as hot as a white flame his eyes fixed on me as though sighting me up through the cross wire of a gun. I was impaled, hooked like a fish on a hook. I had taken the bait and now I was paying the price. The figure rotated 90° towards the house at the side of him. My neck and eyes jarred within the white flame of the maliciously devilish eyes. The figure now in all its glory started feeling around at the gaps between the bricks. After a few more seconds a nod of achievement rocked the neck of the figure. Whatever it was he was looking for, he had found it. The figure reached for the key hanging there majestically, placed it into the wall and twisted. Almost instantly the wall began initiating a vibrating movement and a marvellous and stunning green light filled the alleyway. The dark figure now for the first time looked satisfied with things as he turned back towards me. He pointed his bony, detangled finger towards the light and stated in a devilish tone *"Come with me."*

Daniel Hollinshead

The Unknown
Voyage - Chapter One

Fire was eating away at my skin. They don't expect me to escape from the raging fire pit they placed me in. They should not have judged me so quickly; from the super strength I had developed throughout my journey this was just a minor event.

Striding my way through the outrageous, burning fire I knew I would be experiencing a new scar for my collection. From the distance I could see a small fragile figure watching my getaway and not alerting any of their people to avoid my escape. Suddenly, the figure came running towards me. At first I was startled by this, but as I became more aware of the figure's face, a familiar face shone back at me.

Her fragile face looked at me with despair. As her pale blue eyes looked deeply into mine, a flash of my past emerged from my mind, of a young woman shouting with anger and walking away in a frantic moment of regret without looking back. At that particular scene I remember who this woman who stood in front of me was, my mother. Confusion struck me as my mind cleared and I studied her more closely. Her long silky green robe had an image of a white eagle present on the back of it. This was the robe of the locals who captured me and placed me amongst the ring of fire.

My feelings went haywire, because this woman was the one who left to travel to distant lands and left my father and me when I was young. Now I knew that my voyage was to find my birth mother, I ran away because my instincts told me to. I ran in different directions because my instincts told me to. It was one of my main priorities to know why I had directed myself through the cave that brought me here, and why I kept going and going until I reached this restless land of abnormal, and insane happenings. Not only had I found my mother but I also found myself.

"Your destiny was to be here Gillis," my mother spoke softly.

"B-b-b-ut I don't understand these people, your people tried killing me. I know for a fact I will not befriend these people, what kind of sick joke is this?"

"I predicted you would be like this," my mother responded.

"Why are you here? Is this the life style you come to now live in?" I asked my mother.

"There is nowhere else to go. This world is where our family originate from. Our ways are this village's ways. This is how it's meant to be. Sorry."

My reaction might have been insulting our family's nature, but I had no other choice, living in that rebellious existence was way beyond my limits.

Since being in these infuriatingly poor excuses of a world where people lived, I had discovered a talent that ran in my family, but by the look on my mother's face when I performed it, it was like forbidden to act upon. As I watched over the horizon, in the gloomy sunset, a large, terrorizing copper creature flew over to me like a roaring hurricane. Approaching us my mother went to run, but I had a tight grip on her and there was no way I was releasing her. My rage was uncharacteristic for my nature. My mother was aware of this and struggled no more. I could hear all the commotion in the village. In the midst of the excitement muffled screams were shouting

"Dragon, dragon!"

I approached the dragon cautiously weary of its magnificent powers, but I also exposed that I could influence the dragon's abilities earlier on in my expedition. From this I climbed on the dragon's back with my mother. As we flew into the shadows of the night, my adrenaline pumped faster, and faster, as I knew I was the one controlling this mythical creature.

We arrived at the peak of an unsurprisingly hot mountain. I suspected that I was standing amongst a blistering, living rage of a volcano. My mother seemed timid when she dispatched the fiery creature.

"Dim-witted, irrational fool," my mother spoke in a faint tone. The journey had seemed to make her flimsy figure tired.

"You will thank me in a few decades," I replied with a comfortable manner.

"How can we escape this distasteful world?" I asked.

"From the predicament you have placed us in, we can not be returned to the village, due to that repulsive creature burning it down." As this point was raised, the dragon roared up in fury and blew a large, fiery breath up towards the air. My mother was not frightened at this like she knew the dragon, and how temperamental it could go like the back of her hand. With this she carried on passing a filthy look at the dragon:

"We will have to travel to the furthest side of the land. We need weapons to defend ourselves from the land's deathliest creatures. Make clothes, because this will be a very long journey. If we find ourselves at the end of it, there will be a ghastly, dark cage similar to the one you mentioned earlier. When we carry along inside this cave we will reach very different lands!"

I had nothing to say. It was our only option. We got a handful of sleep. Then we started preparing for our next voyage. I was not alone this time. I was with my mother who was an unassuming, but very strong character.

Lydia Lowe

The Mysterious Animal Life

It was cold and foggy on this one late September morning. It was 2.38am and nobody was to be seen or heard. Nobody that was, except a nocturnal grey farm owl who answered to the name of Hoot. His feathers were very dull and sandy coloured and the texture of them was smooth and firm. Hoot was a very timid barn owl that had a nasty accident last year. Unfortunately, he was housed in a particular barn where a fire had taken place and had only just managed to survive.

The owner of the barn decided to move Hoot into a barn, which had never been used before and all it had inside was a stack of hay. Hoot looked quite happy and content in his barn until he saw a little hole in the back of it. Hoot flew through the hole and the next minute he knew, he was under water with sharks and submarines passing beneath him. To say he was an owl, his faced screwed up like a misshapen ball of paper as soon as he saw the sea creatures and objects around him.

He sat in amazement as seven creatures approached him under the bright blue seabed. There was a bang and a great big splash of water. In a matter of seconds, a sea monster, that was as ugly as an old witch with warts and had a personality as high as a soaring bird came right into Hoot's face.

Hoot leaned back in disgust and flapped his wings as hard as he could to warn the sea monster away. But he wasn't going anywhere. The two of them were sat on the seabed staring when all of a sudden, Hoot said his first words.

"Hey dude!"

The sea monster replied with -

"Yo!" and he made a gun shape with his claws. The two of them put their wings around each other and bounced off through the current of the ocean!

Chelsea Cox

Air Raid

I lay in my bed thinking about how much I enjoyed life before the Germans attacked. I could remember when I heard the first air raid siren I was really scared and I didn't know what to do. That siren was to let us know that the war had begun. I was only nine at the time. I'm twelve now, but that doesn't stop me from feeling unsafe. All I want to do is protect my sister, my mum and dad, but that isn't the reality. I can't protect them from bombs guns and missiles. Before the war I would play outside, conkers mainly, in conker season anyway and I'd always collect the most. Tom got a lot too, but Rick was careful which ones he picked. He'd go for quality not quantity. That's why he pretty much always won. I really miss playing games like that with the lads. I haven't seen any of the lads since that first air raid siren. Tom's mum doesn't let him out and Rick got evacuated somewhere near the coast. It's meant to be really nice there, but he had to travel really far on a train all by himself. Rick was my best friend; Tom didn't really come out much. That's why it was mainly Rick and I. Well soon I'll be getting evacuated. Mum has to start working for the pilots on Monday so I have to go to somewhere in Cornwall.

Monday came quicker than expected and at 5:00am I had begun my long journey from London to Cornwall. I miss my family already. I'm looking forward to being near the sea and sand and sun for a change, because the last trip I had was when I was six. I travelled to a nice cottage in the countryside where we went to grow some plants and find out all about nature. The woman who owned the house was some friend of mum's.

I arrived at the Cornwall station with my small bag of belongings and stood at the corner was an old woman with a cage in her left hand and a sign in her right hand saying 'Bill Tanil.' That was me, why was she holding my name? I slowly walked up to her. She looked pretty normal and wore clothes typical of those that my mum would wear.

"*Hello,*" I said. "*Are you Miss Grimble?*" She looked at me strangely. "*Who wants to know?*" she said in an evil voice, a very evil voice. Oh no. I just couldn't get the picture out of my head cooking and cleaning and doing Miss Grimble's chores. Her evil tone of voice rang through my head like a bell that couldn't stop ringing, a broken record playing over and over. So I answered her question –

"*Bill Tanil, marm,*" I said in a shy, nervous sort of voice.

"*Well, in that case hi I'm Miss Grimble. You are going to be living with me. I'm not like most mums. I don't know much about cooking and cleaning, but I know everything about fun.*" At this point I was really confused. Her tune had totally changed. She went from being the wicked witch of the west to Old Mother Hubbard.

As we were walking down the road breathing in the fresh air (which was just that, no smoke, no bomb fumes just fresh air,) Miss Grimble said –

"*Oh and by the way I'm not into all of that Marm business. Just call me Miranda and I'm sorry for how I spoke to you earlier. I just talk to strangers like that to scare them away.*"

I looked up with a grin on my face and we both burst out laughing. That's when I realized that I was wrong earlier. I was going to enjoy it here so I decided to tell her and she really seemed happy that I felt like that.

"There are thirteen other children at home waiting for you. They are really excited to meet you," said Miranda. *"You'll like them."*

"How old are they?" I said worrying slightly.

"Age range from two to thirteen and all are nice kids and yes I adopt. They're not all mine," she said with a smile on her face and as she said it I noticed a twinkle of pride. *"And here it is the place I like to call home."* As she said that Miranda looked pleased with her home, so I turned to see what was so good about it.

"WOW it's amazing." It was less a house, more a mansion and as I walked up the red bricked paving path that lay neatly underneath my feet, I felt happy and comfortable and safe. These were feelings that for some time had been very infrequent.

"Well," Miranda said in a humorous way. *"I need somewhere for my fourteen children and six cats to stay. Oh and don't forget me,"* her smile was a full of love and joy.

"Cats! I've always wanted a cat," I replied with excitement.

"Well, now you've got six."

At this point my smile was so wide across my face even when I wanted to stop smiling, I couldn't.

She opened the door slowly and commented in a more serious tone –

"Never go into the room across from bathroom three" and then she let me into her house. Stood there were three little girls aged between five and seven.

"They're here! The new boy's here everybody!" screeched the girl, the one that looked so sweet and innocent in a high pitched ear hurting scream. I covered my ears. The floor began to shake underneath me and suddenly a stampede of ten people and six cats came charging at high speeds towards me. Miranda whistled and the whole group lined up.

"Yes Miranda." They behaved very obediently. She went down the line and gave me all their names - Judy, Millie, Molly, Ryan, Tom, George, Graham, Timmy, Joan, Jill, John, Alison, Joanne and then the cats' names.

SIX MONTHS LATER

Yes, they were obedient children and I had a nice time, but something just didn't feel right. They were a lot of fun, but as soon as Miranda came in they were good, boring and obedient and then this one summer's day Miranda came in and everything she told them to do they did. I noticed however that all the children's left eyes winked straight at the same time.

As I was in the shower I was thinking about the whole winking business and as I stepped out of the bathroom, I also remembered the forbidden room. I stood at the long thin door that towered over my head. Why weren't we allowed in this room? It didn't add up. I thought about taking John with me, but then I remembered that if we were to get caught they would quite happily tell Miranda what we were doing so I decided to go alone.

I opened the door and crept down the stairs. It was dark and it smelt like a school science lab after a chemical reaction had gone terribly wrong. I reached the bottom of the winding stairs and lit a candle for light.

What a surprise it was a science lab, but why was there a science lab in the centre of a family home? As I wandered around I noticed pieces of paper in a desk draw. They read as follows:

Insert the chip into the left eye,
Make a small cut at the top of the head,
Place mirrors to divert brain signals,
Then place wig on head,
Finally use "forget that" gas,
Do opposite to reverse.

As the terrible truth dawned on me I ran upstairs to the dormitories and it was true they were all wearing wigs and had a cut on their heads. I fell asleep missing just one vital piece of the puzzle.

When I awoke the next morning, I found myself back in the science lab with Miranda staring at me.

"You've been a naughty boy. I have higher surveillance on you, as you think you know. So now you have made me move your obedience processing forward by six months."

What Miranda had not understood was that the whole of the children were now ordinary children again, not robots, because of the great heroic thing I had done while the children were asleep. The chip was getting lowered closer to my eyes. The children all burst in.

"Get out you know the rules," but they did not budge. *"Children, I order you!"* They kept coming closer.

"No" they replied. Without any warning, they ran

and grabbed Miranda and tied her down to the lab table.
As George untied me Tom commented –

"Bill the honour is yours" and I followed the instruc-
tions. With a small tweak added I caused her to become
the perfect mum....

Two hours later the mailman came to tell me the war was
over and that I should catch the next train home. I did
just that and the thirteen children, six cats and perfect
mum lived happily ever after, as did the Tanils. They
regularly visited each other and I treated the children as
my own brothers and sisters. The only people who knew
about these happenings through the war, were the people
involved and those who went on to read the story.

Emily Kerry

Tera

Hi I'm Madison. I'm twenty two and I live in London, with my sister Lisa and also her boyfriend Malak. So I'm an orphan, but I've been fostered. Thankfully my foster parents are Jack and Claire. The bad thing is that they've got a baby boy, called Josh, but he's just a baby so I don't mind that much. I like to call him baby Joshua, which annoys him so much. I love to do that by the way. So let me tell you about an event, an event so big that it was the biggest event of my life, so far.

Here's how the adventure began...well Lisa (my sister) my foster parents (it was when they had recently adopted me and Liz) and I went to a forest which kind of had an Egyptian air to it... well at least I thought it had at the time. Claire and Jack thought it was a good treat to take us on holiday the second day out of the orphanage. (I was only 14 when this happened) anyway, when we got there, we went inside this weird building. I didn't feel right about this, but no one took any notice.

Liz and I were always looking for adventure especially on this trip. We expected a lot of it. We went into a tunnel that had a straight path, but bent round at the end. Liz was behind me probably looking at her nails, as usual. However, when I turned, Lisa was gone.

"Liz! Liz! Liz?" I shouted, wondering where on earth she could be. If I didn't find her then I was dead! She could be anywhere, plus she didn't know this place! What if she got killed?

"Oh no Liz where are you?" I started whimpering to myself. I heard footsteps coming my way and I quickly hid. The footsteps got closer then fainter again, they had walked in...

"I know you two are playing games." I recognized that voice it was Claire for certain. I was relieved and petrified at the same time.

"The joke's over kids," said Jack.

"Let me get this straight Jack, Liz and I are not kids! We are teens so get your facts straight love. They started whispering to each other. I couldn't figure out what though. Finally they found me."

"Hi Claire. I'm Jack."

"Where is she?"

"I don't know. Where did you last see her?"

"Well Liz and I were coming here. She was right behind me, and when I turned around she was gone."

"I know where she is," a whisper appeared from behind us, but it was not a familiar one. *"My name is Malak. I am from this land, but before I tell you where the girl is, welcome to the forest of mystery. All the people here open their arms to you. I believe that she is called Liz for Lisa; anyway she has found the book. I must go and rescue her before it is too late. It would cause the end of this beautiful forest."*

"So what? Is she gonna die?"

"Yes she would. Does nothing else matter to you?"

"Yeah, is that what you want to hear?" He started to make his way back, but this time more cautiously.

"Wait! I will come with you." As we walked I fainted, for I had a bang on my head, after that bang I fell.

The man Malak was carrying me, when I woke up. I saw a statue of a half man and half beetle!

"What are we doing here and where are we?" I asked.

"Shhh...you must not speak in the great temple of Haruka. We must be quiet, for if we speak we will be

trapped and the temple will be destroyed, but it will not die. We will though and everybody else as well. You had better not make sudden movements or the same will happen. Until we die we would be servants." My belly rumbled!

"I'm hungry! Opps..." I bellowed. I could tell something good was going to happen.

The roof started to crumble like a cookie being eaten.

"Why did you yell and why so loud? Are you ever gonna listen to me? Oh good lord I am making it worse. Time for us to go," he grabbed my arm and pulled me out of the temple. We went through all the rooms. We met Claire and Jack. We quickly rushed through the story blah blah, so we finally got out of that stupid thing. Boy was I glad that I was out of there! Jack and Claire went to a hotel. I whined as I said goodbye.

"Where are we sleeping?" He pointed at an empty space. *"Nah! I'm not gonna sleep there. What are we gonna do now because I'm not sleeping there?"* I spoke still gasping.

"Well, the first thing we would already have been to your sister if you hadn't have yelled. Then we could have all gone home. Plus we all would have had a happy ending. Now either shut up and listen, or go home and talk all, you want. Take your pick."

"I'll shut up," I said quickly.

"Good, now I will get some things for where we are going to sleep tonight. Good thing for you I'm a good builder. You go and start some fire." He went off and came back with branches, a knife and some BIG leaves. He went to a tree, cut all the middle of the trunk out, put branches together as a door and then laid out the leaves to make it more comfortable. He made a quick fire in the

middle. We then slept. Next morning we went back to the dreadful temple.

He went to the thing that is called Haruaka. I think you pronounce it like that. This time Malak pushed its nose, but before we went into the thing he wrapped a cloth around my mouth. When we got in I fainted once again! Yet again I was somewhere else. When I awoke I saw a tub that stood in front of me. The tub as Malak explained may only be used once. He made it clear that it was dangerous. Nobody could even use it more than once. It didn't work! So Malak and I had to find another way. We slowly began walking back to the house. We rested about five hours only. So the next morning I was very tired. I next went to the lake to get washed. When I returned, Malak was gone. I looked everywhere but the temple so I had to go there. After I went into the temple I found him. I looked upon him carefully. He looked different in a way. Then he jumped really high. I mean if he were to do the long jump he would have won by a mile.

"*La, lu, ten, Tera,*" so you know what I did next. I booted him and ran. When I returned he was back to normal. In my mind I couldn't help but think of the words that he said. I asked him about the meaning of tera though. He said that it was the book of the undead. Yeah, it was very freaky. We walked along a path but then it split into two. I went to the left and he chose the right. The path I took was terrifying and difficult, because it had rocks and everything like that. I saw fire in the distance. I ran towards it, but right in the middle of the fire was a ruby. As I walked towards it, the ruby turned black...

Savina Lubika

George And The Giant

Once upon a time there lived a young boy called George. George was quite a shy boy and he had no friends. But one day that all changed.

One day in the summer holidays he went for a walk in the woods. He was travelling for a while and he found a cave. George had never seen this cave before which was very strange because he came to the woods quite often. It was like it had only just appeared, but of course he knew that was impossible so he carried on walking. George had been walking for about another five minutes when he heard a long loud sigh coming from the cave.

"*I must be imagining things,*" he said to himself. So he carried on walking. Not so long after he heard the sigh again. This time he didn't ignore it, he turned round and started walking back towards the cave.

When he arrived at the cave, he looked inside and he saw a big tall shadow. The shadow moved and it made George jump. Although George was a shy boy, he wasn't really that scared (like everyone thought) so he walked further into the cave. When he got to the centre of the cave he saw a giant sat on a very tall tree stump. As George got closer he noticed that the giant was crying. The giant turned round and saw George. As quickly as he could George ran out of the cave. The giant ran after him and shouted –

"*Don't worry I won't hurt you!*" George stopped and turned round. He looked up at the giant towering above him.

"*Hi my name is Tom,*" said the giant. "*I won't hurt you. I just want a friend. You see being so big everyone just thinks I am a weird scary giant.*" A tear fell down Tom's face. George felt sorry for him and he said –

"*Okay! I will be your friend.*" Tom's frown turned into a smile.

"*Do you want to come into my house and have some hot chocolate?*" Tom beamed. So off the two friends went to Tom's house.

When they entered the house Tom told George to sit on the log while he got them a drink. The log was too high for George and no matter how much he struggled he just couldn't get on the log. When Tom came in from the kitchen he picked George up and placed him on the log. When the hot chocolate was done they sat together on the log and George told Tom all about himself.

"*My name is George and I am nine years old. I live with my mum because my dad died before I was born. I have no brothers and sisters, but I do have a dog. He is my only friend.*" George took a long breath he had never told anyone about his life before.

"*Not any more,*" said Tom.

"*What?*" said George looking puzzled.

"*Your dog isn't your only friend any more, because you have me,*" Tom replied. "*Now I am your best friend!*" They smiled at each other. It was then that they knew that they were going to be the best of friends forever.

The next day, George went back to see Tom. Today was the day that their adventures would begin. When George got there Tom was eating his breakfast. He was having ten pieces of toast and butter with a cup of tea. (You see two slices of toast would go in a second for a giant.) George wondered how he would make all this, because it would be a bit difficult to have electricity in a cave. Anyway that didn't matter.

"Hello," said George. He walked into the cave and sat on the floor waiting for Tom to lift him up onto the log. When Tom had finished his breakfast he didn't lift George onto the log like he had hoped instead he put on his coat and said –

"Let's go for a walk." So off they went.

"Where are we going?" asked George.

"We are just going into the woods." When they reached their destination they sat down and Tom reached into his bag and got out loads of food. Then he got out a picnic sheet.

"LUNCH!!!" Tom shouted. So the two of them dug in to the huge meal. George was full after a few bites so Tom ate the rest. Once they had finished their meal they set off walking again.

George had never been in this part of the woods before and he was amazed. It was full of flowers and lots of wonderful animals. There were badgers, rabbits, birds, squirrels and loads of horses in the fields. Then George noticed one horse that was miles bigger than all the rest, even big enough for Tom. Then George thought that the horse might actually be Tom's so he asked –

"Tom is that big horse yours?"

"Yes," replied Tom and they walked over the field to the giant horse.

"What is she called?" George asked.

"Her name is Sally!" said Tom as he climbed onto the horse and pulled George on in front of him. As they were riding the horse George was so scared he thought he was going to fall off.

"What if I fall off?" George asked.

"Then Sally will stop. She is trained you see. If someone falls off, she knows to stop." Those comments made George feel a lot better. They rode Sally all the way back to Tom's house. When they got there they had their tea and then George went home. When he got home his mum asked him where he had been all day.

"At my friend's house," George replied. You see George knew that if he told his mum then she wouldn't believe him, because the thing that George hated the most was when someone didn't believe him. George never planned on telling his mum ever.

Twenty years passed by. There was a good thing and a bad thing about this. The good thing was that George and Tom remained best friends, but the bad news was that George's mum died and he never did tell her that he was a best friend with a giant.

Zoe Clayton

'Golitha' by Mark Denton, 2008

A World Of My Own

"*I hoped with all my heart nobody knew about the garden except me because this wonderful place I had just discovered could be the place I had been looking for. It could be a world of my own.*"

A World Of My Own

I had been up all night thinking and dreading the next day. My boarding school head teacher had told me that it was urgent that I returned home. As I gazed out of my dorm window, I could hear the trees whispering among themselves, the flowers opening up to a new day. A sudden urge of happiness emerged from inside me as the fresh scent of morning air met my nose. I was going to miss Green Hill boarding school. Green Hill had been my second home and I had enjoyed every minute I had spent there. This was the place I had learnt so many things and where I had been involved in so many midnight feasts and adventures. All the special times I had were written as memories in my diary so I could look back at the good times when I had returned home. I wasn't bothered if any of my family read my diary, as they wouldn't believe anything I had written anyway. After all, they weren't special like I was. I had a gift and at first I was unsure how to use it, but I learnt how to and I realized what had been opened up before me.

My last day at Green Hill went so fast as I visited all the places I adored so much. I felt an ache in my heart. I didn't want to leave Green Hill, I wanted to stay here forever and ever, around the ones I loved and cherished. I had spent most of my life here and I didn't understand the urgency of my immediate return home and as I placed the last of my possessions into my black suitcase an overwhelming sensation of emotion over-took my body and I burst out into a flood of tears. My body shaking, I felt hopeless; I didn't want to re-turn home to a place where my own family didn't love me. It would probably be one of my mother's spur of the moment decisions to bring me back home only for me to be sent straight back again. It was like being in a world of my own, where nobody cared or even no-ticed me.

Watching the raindrops trickle down the car window and the beautiful scenery flashing before my eyes left my mind feeling unsettled. I had an anxious sensation growing inside me. Pulling up the gravelled drive, I stared at my home. I didn't feel anything towards it; it didn't feel like a home to me. I stepped out of the car and made my way up the big stone steps, gazing at the stone house. Ivy was creeping up the house and around its many windows. Pots filled with fresh flow-ers were on the pathway to the huge, wooden door that stood before me. Every step I took became more and more make believe, as I knew my family didn't want me here.

The chauffeur strolled past me opening up the gigantic door, revealing a magnificent hallway full of crystal marble and shiny surfaces. Artistic paintings hung on the walls and a tall grandfather clock stood, ticking away at the top of the marble staircase. The hallway I stood in reminded me of a big Masquerade ball and there I was in the middle of a ball wearing a beau-tiful dress that reached all the way to my toes. My dress was a fairytale dress, white and a silvery, greyish blue. My mask, covering my face was the same colours with elegant feathers and bows. Half of my hair was pinned up and the rest curly, cascading down my back. Taking a step forward, the heel of my white shoe made a noise on the marble floor and the soft sound of my trailing dress followed me as I walked into a room full of women and men wearing frilly dresses and formal suits. As I picked up a glass of champagne a blond haired male started towards me and from behind me I heard a faint voice. It was at that moment in time that I was brought back down to earth and I realized that the chauffeur was standing before me.

"*Ere, excuse me young lady, are you listening to me, you were just completely ignoring me. The Lord and Lady would like to see you in the grand dining room immediately and no more daydreaming please. We will have no misbehaviour from you!*" he said in the most unpleasant voice I had ever heard. How dare he speak to me like that? Didn't he know I was part of this family? In a nice, soft and sweet voice I replied –

"*I am so sorry sir my imagination can sometimes just take over. I wonder have you got an imagination? Actually don't bother to answer that, the answer is probably no, living in this household. Cheer up sir, it may be raining, but look on the bright side of life, it's warm and dry in here and I bet you get paid for sitting in the house for the rest of the afternoon. You my friend should feel sorry for the gardener. Anyway good day to you, thank you for bringing me home. Bye.*" Setting off down the hall I looked back. The chauffeur left with a look of disgust.

I turned and walked down the corridor that was on my right and went down it. I halted at the first door to my left. Slowly I placed my hand on the door handle and turned. I gulped at the prospect of facing my family. Stepping into the large room, sat at the table were my mum, dad, my brother Ben and eldest brother Tyler. There in the arms of my mother was a small baby. The baby was wearing a white and pink baby grow. The baby was very cute. I finally clicked on to why I was stood in the family dining room; it wasn't because they had missed me but because they wanted to introduce me to the new arrival. I was out of the picture now, I mean I wasn't really in it to start with but I was totally gone. I didn't understand why I was such a disgrace to them and as I scanned the faces of my family, fake smiles were plastered on each of their faces as if they were delighted I had returned home. I bet they were. I turned, slammed the door behind me and ran outside, teardrops running down my face.

I made my way across the garden at a slow pace taking in the fresh scent of the garden air, and the newly pruned bushes. Stopping, over in the far corner of the garden I noticed a wall covered in ivy. I ran all the way to the wall, going round the dug over borders and under the gigantic Willow tree near the Lake. Over at the wall, looking closely, I saw a barely visible door. Pulling the ivy away from it I gripped the handle and pushed. I wasn't thinking that the door would budge; I fell flat onto my face into the doorway of what looked to be the path leading to a garden. Peering into the garden I saw that it was the most magnificent garden I had every seen with waterfalls and birdbaths. Water features casually dotted around.

The garden took my breath away. I hoped with all my heart nobody knew about the garden except me because this wonderful place I had just discovered could be the place I had been looking for. It could be a world of my own.

Jasmine Hopper

'Chalk-Cliff' by Mark Denton, 2008

Riko

"As I walked on the cliff side the warm air mixed with a cold breeze sent a strange feeling down my spine. As I looked down the cliff side I saw the destroyed village of Ilk hidden below a lower mound of rock."

Riko

As I walked on the cliffside the warm air mixed with a cold breeze sent a strange feeling down my spine. As I looked down the cliffside I saw the destroyed village of Ilk hidden below a lower mound of rock. I was glad I had left the village but then a horrendous thud was heard as the ground shook in front of me. I carried on ahead curious to find out what it was.

Cautiously moving ahead I could just make it out, because at this point thick fog had appeared. With my clothes ripped and the nearest village destroyed everyone now knew what had destroyed the innocent village, it was Asla the dragon but why? As I carried on down the cliffside I was out of breath, but I suddenly stopped at the huge mound in front of me. Looking up I realised it was a dragon; it was Riko, Asla's son.

Accepting that a dragon was in front of me I said to Riko –
"What are you doing here?" He told me that his father had planned to destroy the village because the dragon slayer in that village had killed his other son Juto, Riko's brother, but Riko refused to destroy the village because other people in the village were innocent so his father attacked him!

Later on Riko managed to find the strength to get up from the ground. He was cut all over at that point. I remembered that I saw a piece of torn clothing further up the cliffside. I told him to stay there as I rushed to get the piece of clothing. I picked it up and quickly ran back. Coming back towards Riko I looked down to see Asla scouting the area. I thought to myself what was he doing here, but I carried on running. I finally reached back to Riko.

I tied the clothing around Riko's gash on his leg. I looked at him in a puzzled way,

"*Erm... your dad is here and I think he's looking.........*"

"*Look out!*" Riko shouted as he interrupted me. I looked up and saw a figure, which came clearer as it came closer, it was a very furious dragon Asla, and I quickly gathered that he must have seen me running across the cliffside.

I suddenly sprinted past Riko. I had to dodge the fireballs, and the anger of each fireball grew as it hit the ground. I knew that I had to keep going, but suddenly I ran out of the path. Thankfully I stopped in time as my toes were hanging off the edge of the cliff.

I looked back to see Riko and Asla. As they came closer they had growing anger in their eyes.

"*I told you not to talk to humans,*" growled Asla to Riko. Next thing Riko was thrown to the ground with such a force...he didn't move...he was dead. Asla had killed his own son and I was his next target. I nervously looked over the edge to see there was a river at the bottom of the very steep cliff!

The next few moments came in a blur but then Asla looked very wrathful! I made a run for it with Asla firing at me then all of a sudden the path collapsed...

Janina Sills

'Sycamore' by Mark Denton, 2008

The Abyss

"*I was surrounded by a cold darkness; the coldness attacked my face like a pack of wolves scratching into my skin. There was nothing apart from a small sycamore tree growing between the two mounds. I felt small vibrations from the east.*"

The Abyss

The sun shone brightly as my eyes struggled to peer through the battling glare of light. The trees swayed and ruffled in the wind. A dark figure, of which rumours had been spread around towns about, appeared in front of me. As it approached I felt my body temperature rise and its bone-melting stare fell upon me. It looked like a human connected to a wolf. I pulled out my bone-blaster, my favourite weapon. It had seen many deaths; I took aim but one second too late. It grabbed me by the arm and raised me to its eye level. Its breath sickened my three stomachs. I threw my fists at it, but it was no use. Even though I was fifteen foot in height, I looked as short as a leprechaun compared to the size of this hideous beast. I finally managed to break free. I built strength in my four legs and ran as swift as possible. The passing air cooled my face. The valley appeared with its black emptiness in the dip, which I had to pass to get to safety. The weather suddenly changed, it began to rain and thunder. A sudden flash made me run into the dark abyss.

I was surrounded by a cold darkness; the coldness attacked my face like a pack of wolves scratching into my skin. There was nothing apart from a small sycamore tree growing between the two mounds. I felt small vibrations from the east. I turned around to find a rachef drooling down my back. The rachef are always terrorising our towns. They are huge eight-legged beasts that could tear a building to pieces within seconds.

The rachef's eight eyes stared into mine and left an almighty cold chill in my spine. I tried to run but my legs were glued to the floor. It picked me up to its jaws and revealed its ten rows of teeth. I closed my eyes and prepared to die until the half-man half-wolf appeared out of nowhere and tore the rachef to pieces. An all-powerful roar flooded the valley and the vibrations were similar to that of a small earthquake. The thing picked me up and threw me on its back and began to run. I turned and saw the hideous beast towering upon us.

The repulsive beast stared upon me with its eight hideous eyes. The size of the monster made me look like an armadillo. The eight hirsute legs stomped furiously as the queen rachef gave chase. I found my bone-blaster buried in the thick coat of fur of the beast that was carry-ing me. I took aim at the rachef's head and fired. Green slime flew everywhere as the savage monster's head exploded into a thousand pieces. The thing I had been saved by said it was a wolfan, an almost extinct species. After a few hours travel I arrived home and began telling you of my adventure into the abyss.

Jordan Cockles

Yelrebmik

The villagers of Notelgnah still called it the Whishger house even though it had been many years since the family had lived there. It stood on a hill overlooking the village of those more unfortunate than them. All the entrances and windows had been blocked off from any sunlight or anything for that matter. Tiles were missing off the rough tiled house and ivory and wild flowers had over taken the side of the house. Once before there had been miles of huts and houses surrounding the up coming fields filled with flowers and animals on the farms where the sun shone on the whole village. Now however Whishger house was a damp, old building falling to bits and the view was of some old houses still in their places with the different families coming and going.

The fields had turned into mud baths and wild plants surrounded the miles of weeds. All the villagers agreed that the old house was spooky and they still believed that someone or something was still in there.

A century ago something strange and horrible had happened. The story had been picked over so many times and had been embroiled in so many places that nobody was quite sure what the truth was any more. But every version that everyone came up with was all the same place: fifty years before the present day, at daybreak on a warm summer's morning when the house was well kept and impressive, a maid had entered the living room to find all of the Whishger dead.

The maid ran screaming and crying hoping that this was some kind of joke. As she screamed she could feel her lungs tightening up and her legs starting to feel like lead. She felt herself falling over. She ran in to the grocery shop and they questioned her in disbelief.

"*What did you say? What did you say?*" and "*Who's dead? Who is it? Speak girl, speak.*" The maid told them what she saw.

"*They were laid in their places still wearing their dining clothes at the table with their ice cold eyes still open as if they had been there for days. They all had the exact same marks on their bodies.*"

The police were summoned and the whole of little Notel-gnah were surprised and shocked with curiosity and ill-disguised excitement. Nobody wasted their breath pretending that the family was loved, because truthfully it could have been anyone who killed them. Everyone hated them, because they didn't care about anyone else except themselves and their money and they wouldn't let anyone get in between them.

As the weeks went by nobody knew what, by whom or why that family had been killed. They just assumed that it was because of their money and who they were. The police still had no idea about anything. It had been so strange, because there was no evidence to say that the maids or anyone in the house did it or anyone from the outside did the crime. All they knew was that there were three murders at lunch time in the Whishger house and no evidence to prove it. There were no foot-prints and no handprints on the bodies, or anywhere else in the house.

Years went by and still no one knew anything so the police were taken off the case and it was left as a question to everyone about what really happened that day, a mystery murder they called it. No one could do anything about it because of the lack of evidence. What they didn't know was that one of the oldest maids who worked there was the mother of a well-known creature in that area called Yelrebmik.

It lived under the village and when the family made the maid angry she stomped four times and screamed with such a high-pitched voice that humans couldn't hear her. The only one who could hear her was her son. Everyone in the village didn't know the son of the mother, because he didn't come out often and he lived under the houses. He was born a couple of years before the same happened to another family who were murdered. They just blamed it on the maid because her hair was in the dinner. One thing that both families had in common was that they were both filthy rich.

This happened for the rest of the year until one of the other maids saw her with Yelrebmik and screamed and ran out the door straight down to the police and told them what she had seen. They thought that she was crazy as her temperature shot up and she was out of breath as her whole body felt as though it was burning. The police went straight down to the house and saw the monster.

They all got their guns ready and started to fire at the strange creature and Yelrebmik kept fighting back with his fire breath and stabbing them with his horns. BANG Yelrebmik was shot down. He scorched, as his mum screamed too. They could feel each other's pain. She took him and flew off to the underground. Before she left she screamed –

"This is not over!"

Kimberley Hempshall

The Scare Of Your Life

The young girl gazed at the derelict house; her hands were as cold as ice blocks as she took a step towards it. The leaves under her feet ruffled, the wind soared though her hair. Suddenly, a sinister voice screamed her name. Her heart was beating out of her chest. Maybe it was because she was lost, or maybe it was because no one would listen to her problems. She crept to the front door and creaked it open, taking another step on the dusty and unused floor.

A bloodstained door caught her eye. She twisted the doorknob and pushed it open. Slowly she saw a dining table with three odd chairs around it and a tablecloth, which dangled on the floor. She lifted the Victorian cloth and saw a rotting body. It looked female, but she was not so sure, so she examined the body more closely. Her nose and stomach retched at the deadly rank smell. One thing was clear, however she died, it wasn't pretty.

The girl tried to phone the police but there was no signal. She ran to the front door, but it was locked. She was trapped and now she was even more scared than before. She started to hear footsteps, but she thought it was her mind playing tricks on her. All of a sudden her phone rang. The screen said "unknown" she picked it up. All she could hear down the line was cold, heavy breathing; it gave her such a foreboding terror that she hung up. Now she was alone, alone and cold. The footsteps were hurling towards her. She decided to try to kick the door down, but it didn't work. She started

to panic, all of a sudden she passed out ... . . and that was the end of Kate Liveday.
 R.I.P

Jessica Kitty Wright

Annabella's Mystery

I stepped into the attic. It was pitch black. All I could see was the shining of the old mirror that had been left leaning against the wall scattered with dust. Rats scurried around circling my feet. As I stumbled around I kept knocking into boxes left scattered on the attic floor. Curious to know what was in them, I always used to question my aunts but they wouldn't tell me. I was disappointed but it gave me the chance to imagine what I could find.

I heard my auntie's footsteps getting closer and closer. I quickly tiptoed out of the light coming from the attic steps. I shouldn't have been there. I heard her usual squeaky voice calling my name –

"Annabella, Annabella," she screeched. I ran towards the big brass doorknob and stopped. My aunties had always told me to turn it to the right. Why? Not thinking I turned it to the left...

Suddenly I was within a warm exotic breeze. Where was I? I heard my auntie shouting to me in the background, but it was too late now. I carefully stepped forward into the new world not knowing what would happen next. Fairies fluttered past my face. All I could see was big, green leaves swaying gently in the warm wind. Unicorns galloped towards the beautiful setting sun. Everything was like I had always imagined things in my dreams to be, but it all seemed too good to be true. I walked forward for what seemed ages, until I stumbled and fell over a fallen tree. I heard a gentle twinkling behind me.

I was daydreaming when I was suddenly brought back to reality by something that screamed. I jumped startled by the noise. What could it be? I turned to see a beautiful little creature tugging on my brand new pink dress. I gently pushed it off, placing it lightly on top of a large violet petal. I then realised what it was… a pixie. It came to tell me that something was wrong. I remembered what my aunts had told me, pixies weren't real; they were only real when my dad told me the stories about the wonderful world of mischief.

"*Oii,*" squeaked the little pixie, "*What happened to the apology?*"

"*Oh, sorry, my name is Annabella,*" I curtsied sweetly, "*And yours?*"

The pixie proudly stood up and replied –

"*My name is Trixie, Queen of Pixie Land.*"

I gently shook hands with Trixie; her hand was as small and as delicate as a daisy petal.

The world started spinning around me magically, the air seemed to glimmer pink before my eyes. What was happening? The next thing I knew I had shrunk to the size of a pixie myself. The grass grew over me. Flowers towered over my head, now bigger and more beautiful then ever. I looked over to Trixie; she had a smug look on her face. She had done this. All I could think was how would I get back?

Trixie began to speak –

"*Annabella, do you want to come to my house? Now that we are very good friends?*"

"*Oh, I would be honoured but I really have to get home.*"

"You'll be okay with me and it's only for five minutes."
How could I refuse? I had already stepped on her foot and nearly broken it. I didn't know what to do; I couldn't refuse. But my aunties would be worrying. They were always so very protective of me since my father died. Anyway I do owe the pixie an apology; it wouldn't hurt anything, would it ...

I didn't know what to do so I turned back to Trixie. I was just about to say no when she started mumbling something at me. Unexpectedly she gave me a hug, but as I looked at her, tears were streaming down her little face like shimmering diamonds. Anxiously she started telling me about her life. She told me about her terrible childhood. Her father, the former King, and herself lived together in the palace, but he always had to leave her with her awful aunts when he left for war. Afterwards the word *"YES"* blurted out as fast as you can say the word yes.

The journey to Trixie's house seemed to be miles and took ages, but I couldn't turn back now. I had already promised her. We walked down twisty paths through the woods. Grass lined paths and colourful flowers were scattered everywhere. It was beautiful. When we had finally reached the other side of the woods we got to a big tree blocking our path. This was Trixie's house.

She took me inside and showed me around. Everything was carefully organised and very cosy. Now it was her turn to ask about my life. I didn't know what to say. Should I tell her how I have to live with my awful aunts or not? I didn't want to upset her again. I decided to tell her the truth. Maybe she could help me.

I took a deep breath and started to talk –

"I don't really know what to say, my life hasn't been a very happy one but here goes," I paused to see if Trixie wanted to say anything but she just nodded at me to carry on. *"Well, when I was little I lived with my dad but he died, I was forced to go and live with my aunties but I hate it. They won't let me go out, or do anything. They are too protective. I wish my dad was still alive."* I turned back to Trixie; she had tears in her eyes. *"Are you ok?"* I asked worried I had upset her.

"Yes, I just feel so sorry for you, if there was anything I could do?" she asked looking concerned.

"I don't think there is really is, but it's okay…Wait, there is one thing but…" I paused for a second, *"Tell me, please, I will do anything to make my life happier."* I begged and gave her a persuasive look.

She grabbed me by the hand and led me through the tiny house and up the spiral staircase. I guessed this must be the way to her room. Inside it looked just like my bedroom, pink and purple, my favourite colours. Right at the back of the room was a door on the wall; I wondered where it led to as we were at the edge of the house, unless it was magic. Just as I was thinking to myself she wandered over to the door and started mumbling words to herself and tapped on the door a few times. What was she doing?

She opened the door and just stared in for a few seconds.

"Is this your house," she asked. I stepped forwards to have a look before replying.

"Yes, how did you know?"

"You don't need to know that, the only thing I will say is I've done a little bit of my magic on your aunties." She looked at me with a cheeky grin on her little face.

"You haven't hurt them have you?" I asked anxiously, nervous of what she could have done.

"Don't worry, everything will be OK now, I've just helped them learn how to treat you right."

I felt worried about this, but anything would be better than it was before. Back inside the attic everything seemed the same as when I left. The boxes were still there and the mirror propped up against the wall, but this time it was lighter and a lot cleaner. Now I knew something had happened. I walked across to the attic door; my auntie walked past underneath me. She shouted up to me –

"Annabella come downstairs now, your supper's going cold." I was lost for words. Why hadn't she gone mad at me for being up there? This was amazing. Quickly I ran back over to the secret door I had come from. Trixie was stood in the doorway with a big happy smile on her face and her little head was nodding away at me.

"Thanks," I whispered trying not to let my auntie hear me. I carefully shut the door and went downstairs. I was now happier than ever and knew I always had another friend waiting for me at the other side of the door!

**Katie Callan, Stephanie Shaw,
Jo Annabella Farnell, Zoe Latham**

The Street

As I entered the basement door, a cold shiver ran down my spine. I moved towards the door at the back of the room and my hand slowly urged forward. I grabbed the door handle and swiftly moved through. Inside, the room was dark, so I couldn't see a thing. I reached my hand out in front of me to feel my way through. I felt a damp wall at the side of me. Following the wall along, I came to the end of an alley.

I came to the opening of a unique looking street. I walked out of the alley and down some steps. It was dark and the streetlights were dim, I turned back up the steps back to the door, there was no door! I screamed for help, there was no way back and I didn't know where I was, I was trapped on a unique looking street in the middle of nowhere!

I had to find my way back but how? Was there another door or a way back to the basement? Was it like a game? Perhaps I had to get to the next level. I was unsure. I walked back down the steps and into the street. The row of houses at the side of me looked derelict. I walked further down the street. As I was walking, a putrid smell entered my nose; it was the smell of death. I looked around, but I saw nothing. My legs were shaking and my palms were sweaty, but still, I walked on. The smell was getting stronger, until, it was as though, I was the smell. I looked around, I caught a glimpse of something, an animal, it wasn't moving but it was breathing heavily. I urged forward. The creature was black with a tuft of fur on its back. I bent down to get a closer look. The creature looked wounded. I had never seen anything like this before.

The smell was sickly and I had to cover my mouth to avoid vomiting. I moved round to the front of the creature. To my horror, it was bleeding, its teeth were razor sharp and were covered in blood, it looked like a dog but it was as big as a horse! I touched the creature, it flinched, and then it moved. My heart was pounding so fast, I thought it would explode. The creature opened its bloodshot eyes, and mustered a cold stare at me. Then, the creature began gasping for air. I stood to my feet and looked around, the entire street was filled with hundreds of dead creatures. What were they? Werewolves? I had to find out more...

Jordan Hutchinson

The Nightmare World

Night-time fell. The air turned bitter and the wind turned fierce. The old abandoned graveyard was just seconds away. We pulled up our jackets close to our chests and set off.

We came to the entrance. Carefully but silently we opened the tall metal fence with the signs that read 'NO TRESPASSING' and 'BEWARE'.

I turned and looked at her, as if to say 'Are we going through or turning back?' In the end we went through. Did we make the right decision?

We stepped onto the long and narrow path of the grave-yard. We walked quickly but firmly, as the darkness seemed to creep upon us. It felt like someone or some-thing was behind us, following us, watching us. Our spines began to shudder and our hearts beat faster. They were the only things we could hear.

Hurrying along, we noticed an old wooden door. It seemed like it had been there for years. The wood was rotting and the hinges were rusting. We approached it carefully, as we didn't know what was on the other side. We reached forward, placed our shaking hands on the old rusting handle and pulled it down. We exchanged looks. What was in store for us?

Walking steadily through the door we watched where we placed our feet within the darkness. We couldn't see our trembling hands, even when they were right in our faces. We began to panic. Were we in danger? Should we turn back?

We carried on; feeling our way through. The normal things seemed different. The spiky, prickly branches were scratching our bare arms. The owls hooted in the trees above and bats flew over our heads. The trees were watching our every move. I quickly became scared. I had no idea of what my best friend was thinking but I knew it had to be the same.

A light came out of the darkness and shone on our faces. Relieved that we weren't in the darkness our fear was beginning to fade, the wind was calming down. Our eyes became droopy with tiredness. In the end we found a place to rest for the night. Somewhere where we could escape from all of this. The place kept us separate from the madness of our day.

We awoke at the crack of dawn. The distant sound of a scream could be heard. We jumped up with fear, palms sweating and hearts pounding. The noise began to come closer. Fearing for our life, we ran to escape from the terrifying sound. I turned around. She was gone!

All alone now, I had to find her. I set off running through the woods, scared and lonely. The normal noises began to scare me, twigs snapping, birds tweeting it didn't seem right. The whistling wind was gradually growing stronger. As I ran, I came across something that made me stop. It was an old skipping rope with pretty pink tassels, just like the one she had when she was little but lost. I couldn't stop thinking how it got there. Was someone stalking us? Did this explain who might have taken her or where she might have gone?

I picked up the skipping rope anxiously, determined it wasn't hers. At least I hoped it wasn't. Unfortunately it was. Our names were written on both handles in red ink. I admired the rope repeatedly just to make sure I wasn't seeing things, but again I wasn't. My heart thumped against my fragile chest. It felt like it was going to thump right through my cold pale skin.

I steadily walked on, through the bare bushes and the tall trees. My mind started to fail me. All bad thoughts ran wild in my mind. I didn't know what to do. I couldn't take this anymore. I wished this was all a dream and I could wake up next to her. She would tell me everything was okay, but this was not a dream. This was completely real.

Suddenly, the scream could be heard again. Even though I had no idea of who it might be, I just knew it had to be my best friend. I pulled myself together, got over the bitter cold air, over the numbness of my fingertips and cheeks and ran towards the poor innocent screamer. What if someone was purposely leading me to the scream so I would follow it and be completely fooled that it was my best friend?

As I came closer I saw a highly erect dark figure. He was stood beside a tree that was stood all on its own. He was holding something or someone. It was too hard to tell what it was from where I was. The figure started to walk away from me still holding that something in his hand. He stopped. Something deep down was telling me it was him.

I looked at his back. He turned. Faced me. He started to walk in my direction. He stopped once again, and then turned away as if he had to be somewhere. Where was he going?

He walked in the direction of the woods where it was gloomy, terrifying and spine chilling. I found it hard to keep up with him. I was concentrating on where he was heading and I tripped over and screamed. The figure turned around and looked directly into my eyes. He dropped whatever he was holding. I couldn't wait around and be his next victim. I quickly picked myself up and ran for my life back through the intimidating woods. I could feel his breath on the back of my neck. I just knew he wasn't behind me. My palms started to burn, my head dripping with sweat. I had to hide and get away from this monster. I turned around and he started to run. He was faster than me. He vanished.

I turned around, looking everywhere to make sure he wasn't hiding, ready to jump out on me, take me and never be seen again. I had to keep safe just in case she came back and needed me to look after her. I couldn't leave her alone. I looked up to the sky and noticed a cloud shaped like an arrow. It was pointing behind me. I turned around and the dark figure was lurking there. He had an elderly kind of face. He looked miserable and lonely. I noticed he had blood on his face, right next to his left eye.

He stared at me helplessly. He needed my help. I walked towards him but he backed off, maybe he was afraid.

He turned round, looked at the sky and fell fiercely at the ground. Should I help him? I went over to him, picked him up and leant him against an oak tree. I made sure he was okay then ran.

Running for my life, I didn't seem to care about the things around me. BANG!!! I fell to the ground. I began to look to see who it was. To my surprise it was my best friend. We hugged and got over the surprise.

I moved my arm. It became sticky. Quickly moving it, I found out that it was blood. We were next to a dead body. It looked like the victim had fallen on her head. We managed to get a look at this person. It was a young girl not much older than us. All I could think about was 'I'm glad it wasn't my best friend. How will her family react?'

We had to get out of there or else we might have been the next victims. Everything was so different now. We couldn't understand why this was happening to us, or what was happening. We didn't know how to answer any of our questions; our heads were all shaken up and fuzzy.

We tried to get home but we were lost. There was no other way of putting it. I remembered what my grandma told me once, 'always do what you think is right.'

We went back to check to see if the other victim was alright. He was gone! We were really scared now. We ran, didn't know where, just ran.

Out of nowhere an old wooden door appeared. We recognized it immediately. It was the door we walked through which led here. We were so relieved that we could go home.

The pounding of rain awoke me. I looked to my right then my left. My best friend was laid there next to me. Relieved that it was all over I began to be happy.

Later that day I asked my friend all about it and what happened. She had no idea what I was on about. Was it all a dream?

Megan Robinson

The Magic Door

The hinges creaked and the door moaned as it screeched slowly open. I'd been searching for the key to this door for years and after fifteen years of searching for the key, I'd finally found it. This was the moment I'd been waiting for, for so long. The door swung eerily open to reveal a whole new world. I didn't dare open my eyes to see what was behind it.

As I opened my eyes and stepped forward into the new world I was astounded at the sight before me. The ground was a brown sandy colour and crumbled beneath my feet as I walked forward. The sky was pink and the clouds swept across the sky like an artist's painting. Trees lined the horizon for miles around and a stream of crystal blue water trickled down the middle.

I looked around for some sign of life, I walked forward the sand blowing up beneath my feet and creating soft clouds of dusts like a warm blanket wrapping itself around me. There was deadly silence and no sign of life anywhere. I didn't know what to do. The world I had been dreaming of for years was just an ordinary beach. Nothing out of the ordinary, nothing special just this. I could carry on exploring. But what was the point? I turned towards where the door was, but it was gone and just more sand was in its place. It was like the door never existed I couldn't get out. Was I trapped here forever?

I found a rock nearby to sit on. It was cold and hard but I didn't care. I buried my head in my hands I didn't know how I could escape this world. How was I going to escape? I didn't think I could undo my actions.

A high-pitched wail filled the silent land, I looked up and a horrific sight flooded my vision. The monster's shadow plunged me into the darkness, its body towering over me. Evil red eyes glared down at me. I tucked my legs underneath myself to try and make myself disappear, but it was no use. The monster had green scales and long tusks coming out of the side of its head. He brought his head closer to mine. I could feel its breath whipping my face. I scrunched my eyes up and wished it would all go away. As I opened my eyes the sun came back across my face as the creature turned its back and began to walk away. I breathed a sigh of relief. I looked up and realised I was no longer alone.

The once clear sky was filled with animals with wingspans as long as the masts of the biggest ship. On the floor they roamed freely, I could hear the remote cries of them in the distance. I was in the dinosaur ages.

The door I thought was a trick had taken me back thousands and thousands of years. This was incredible I should have thought this through though, because now I was in a land, alone, with dinosaurs and no idea how to get home. I meandered around aimlessly wondering how I was going to get home. I looked around but there was no sign of the door.

I decided to go back to where the door was. I walked a while and then for a further period of time, trying to remember where the door was. Maybe I shouldn't have come. I shouldn't have looked for the key and got obsessed with the contents of the door. Now I was trapped.

Rebecca Taylor

The Castle Of Cinos

Deep within the frightening, creepy castle stood a girl called Eitak. She was a short and sweet girl who lived within it. She had a friend who lived with her and she was called Yma. Yma was a tall and polite girl who had lived with Eitak for a long time. It was night-time and it was thundering and lightning. The lightning was flashing through the tall windows of the castle; the lightning sounded with really loud bangs.

All the lights went off inside the castle. Yma went to get a candle and lit it. As it flickered she saw a shadow of a mysterious creature in the darkness. The east wing window opened and a cold gust of wind sent a shiver down Eitak's spine. The candle went out, so Eitak came across to Yma and she brought her a lantern. They saw the shadow again so they both started to scream. They looked into the mirror that was on the wall and they saw the man stood there.

Eitak and Yma ran in to another room in the castle and were shouting. They got really scared and they didn't know what to do. They both decided to run out of the huge castle doors. Eitak and Yma were both walking around and then it got to 11pm and the two girls were still outside. They wouldn't go back into the castle in case the man was still there. An hour later they both started to walk back up to the castle, because it was getting too late for them to be out at that time on their own. On the way back to the castle they could feel as if someone was following them.

Eitak and Yma then stopped and turned around, but they didn't see anything so they turned back again and carried on walking. Then they felt something touch their shoulder and they stopped again and saw the man there with his hand on Yma's shoulder. Eitak opened the castle door and they both quickly ran into the castle and shut the door. As they locked the door they both turned round and the mysterious creature was stood there. They thought it was just a dream and there was no man there. So they ignored that the man was there and went upstairs. Yma went in her room and Eitak went to her room. Eitak got into bed. Then there was the man again. Eitak got really scared because the man had been following her and Yma all day. So she shouted –

"*Yma*" and said, "*The man's there again. He's been following us all day.*"

"*Don't be daft it's because you saw him earlier you think that he's there again,*" shouted Yma.

"*No really he has come here to look,*" said Eitak frightened.

Yma got out of her bed and went to Eitak's room but the man had gone, so Yma went back into her own room, but then it appeared again so Eitak shouted again. This time Yma saw the man. Yma and Eitak tried to get out of the room, but the man was stood against the door and wouldn't let them out. The man then moved so Eitak ran out of the room and went to Yma's room. Everywhere she went the man followed her, she was getting really scared. She didn't know why the man was following her everywhere she went. Eitak didn't sleep that night and the next day the man wasn't there. He was gone, but Eitak still didn't know why the man was in the castle and following her everywhere. Then a woman heard the two girls screaming so she followed to where the screaming was coming from and she reached the castle and knocked on the huge castle doors.

Eitak went downstairs and opened the door.

"Would you like to come in?"

"Yes please," said the woman. Eitak then shut the doors of the castle and asked the woman to sit down so she did.

"Who are you and why are you here?"

"I heard screaming so I came to see where it was coming from," she said.

"But who are you?" Eitak asked.

"I also heard people shouting saying there was a man following them and the sound was coming from here." The woman started to explain that she was the man's mum and that he was called Semaj. They had once lived in the castle, but someone had killed Semaj. So she decided that she didn't want to live in such a big castle on her own and so moved out.

The next day Eitak and Yma decided to move out of the castle and move into a normal house because the man was always there. They went upstairs and made sure all the windows were shut. Packing their stuff they went down stairs rang the woman who came to see them before and asked if the woman would take them up to where all the houses were. Eitak and Yma took their suitcase outside and Eitak locked the tall castle doors. The woman then arrived and they got into a car and left.

Katie Fletcher

'Tinmines' by Mark Denton, 2008

The Lucille Monster

"The sinister, spooky, cold-hearted castle stood at the top of the towering and menacing coastline of Lucille. Black clouds soon rolled in as the biggest storm the village had ever witnessed embarked upon them."

The Lucille Monster

The sinister, spooky, cold-hearted castle stood at the top of the towering and menacing coastline of Lucille. Black clouds soon rolled in as the biggest storm the village had ever witnessed embarked upon them. The sound of thunder collided with the castle as the whole village shook with fear.

The monster of the castle came out and the nearby village trembled. His hideous eyes gazed upon the village looking for his next victim of terror. His teeth were as sharp as razors filling every space in his mouth as he gave a devious smile. As he looked down he saw with his red hideous eyes that all of the villagers were running into the shelters to get away from him, from Retsof the monster of the castle in Lucille.

He anxiously pounced down the mountainside going as fast as a wild dangerous tiger, looking and watching. His mouth now wide open with hunger and anticipation, his nose catching the smell of fear, strong fear as the villagers hurried to safety in the many underground shelters of the village. Retsof would get what he wanted. He needed it.

Retsof saw something in the corner of his glimmering red eye. It was a school bus filled with fulfilling young children from the private school of Harrogate. What a shock to see that he was going to make his prize work for the first time in two hundred years and this was the only time he needed it to.

He heard something, something distant, so he clambered up into a tall tree on the mountainside where he could get a perfect view of what was happening. It was dark but with his eyes being red, they glowed and brightened up everything around him and made his task easier to complete. The children were getting off. He watched them, one by one taking in every detail. He shook with an even greater hunger and a sense of what was to happen. Watching closely he saw climbing gear and then realised that they were to climb the mountain of Lucille the next day and go into his castle to sleep that night ... what was he to do?

He got out of the tree and went back up the mountain and into his deadly rotten-stench of a castle and began to scheme and plan how to get them one by one...

The storm continued into the night and early morning. The young children came out of the village hotel petrified and worried about the stories they had seen and read in the hotel wondering if they were true or simply made up to scare them. No this was real and it was happening. Feeling petrified of the castle a child exclaimed -

"I don't want to stay so high in a castle all night it is too much for me yet" so the teacher let him stay on the bus for that night telling him to take care, but unlucky for him he was to be the first.

Retsof gazed down from the top of the mountain licking his lips and clawing the ground with his dreadfully disgusting long nails as he watched from the trees. Suddenly with his sensitive ears he heard the young boy stumble up the bus steps and the doors close behind him.

"Yes" he sneered. His plan of terror had begun.

Then the mayor, white as a ghost, almost petrified of being caught by Retsof was looking out of his shelter shouting to the group –

"*No don't go up there, it's too dangerous,*" but they couldn't hear him so he looked around for Retsof. He wasn't there like he usually was; he had vanished like a magician in a cloud of smoke. As he came out cautiously he began to walk up to the group of children to warn them to get out as they were in grave danger, but things didn't go as planned. Retsof was following; moving behind him...what was to happen?

Alicia Foster

The Nightmare Terror

As I stood as still as a statue, everyone was staring at me with his or her evil eyes. I was scared and felt lonely as the beasts were grinding their teeth at me. The sky was grey and dull, and all around me were millions of people, all men, with tight fitting armour and sharp swords in their big beastly hands.

The silence was peaceful for a moment until....

'*Get Him!!!*' I heard a loud scary voice demanding all his men to kill me. I took a massive gulp; I could feel my stomach churning. I had never been this nervous.

As all the beasts came charging at me I clenched onto my sword. I was thinking hard, should I fight back or should I run? I had to fight for my family and the rest of my men who had left me behind. The shouting and screaming was beginning to hurt my ears. I ran as fast as the speed of light towards these scary men. I was confused, voices in my head wanted to stop me, but others were encouraging me.

Whilst clasping onto my sword, I came face to face with a tall bulky man. Our swords were smashing against each other. I could see the anger in his beady eyes staring at me with disgusting levels of hatred as we were fighting.

Unexpectedly I felt sharp blades nudging my back. I turned around to look who it was, only to find all my men had come back to help me. I wasn't alone, I felt confident and proud to fight now. All the pains in my stomach had suddenly gone.

As everyone charged at each other, the sky turned dull and black, the atmosphere was tense and very scary. I could hear shouting and screaming constantly and I could smell the horrible stench of blood pouring out of the wounds of these animalistic men.

I stood back from all the mess, which I could see in front of me. I sat down and thought of why I had walked through the tree, to come to this nightmare. All I kept thinking was –

"Just go back and leave this nightmare world." Unfortunately there was one big problem stopping me from doing that… How do I get back?

I stood up and ran back to the tree. With sweat dripping from my head I knew I had to keep on running. The door, which had been cut out of the huge old tree, had disappeared. I began to worry.

"Oh no, what do I do?" I thought.

I had to go back to my men. I couldn't be as terrible as them and leave people behind. When I finally arrived back to where the fighting was happening, I was in shock. Silence had broken into the large field. With bloody bodies laid dead on the floor, I slowly walked around to find that all the dead men were my team-mates. Tears began to roll down my face, never before had I been so heartbroken in all my life.

The guilt inside me was unbelievable, why did they come back for me? They came back to help me and I left them. As I left to try and escape rain began to pour down from the dark miserable sky. The field started to come to an end, as I reached the tree again. But the door wasn't there, what was I going to do, how was I going to escape?

Kirsty Booth and Jade King

Unknown World

I ran, ran as fast as I could. I needed to win this race. Suddenly there was a flash of light and I was in a place I had never been before, where the sea was blood and where the ground was littered with the dead bodies of weird creatures. I could not believe my eyes, where could I be...?

I saw a creature, it was alive, and it had fangs dripping with blood. With thoughts of vampires I ran. Suddenly I was falling, falling into a cave.

"*Are you a vampire?*" someone, or something, grunted.

"*No,*" I replied with a groan. Four strong arms picked me up and put me on my feet.

"*It is a human!*" someone said and they all started cheering and shouting - "*The prophecy, the prophecy was true.*" I asked the nearest person –

"*What prophecy?*" and she/he (I couldn't tell which) started explaining to me of a prophecy made long ago by a witch that a human from the other world would appear in the resistance and the human would bring an end to the vampires' ruthless rule over the world.

As the day went by I realised that nearly no one spoke English, they hardly spoke at all actually. I made my own weaponry and they were amazed at what I created. They fought with branches that they had made sharp, whilst I made myself a sword and shield, a spear, a bow and arrow, a mace and pure silver plate body from the ores that they had thrown away believing they were useless. I went on to create a fire which, when certain herbs was added, was like a blazing furnace. I also made fortifications for their base as well as a pure silver neck shield, which was embedded with garlic so if a vampire tried to convert them then the vampire would die instead. We decided to go to a nearby village where there were vampires and a few resistance prisoners who had been caught and were to be converted the next day. An hour later we were making the journey to the village of Immortal where there were three vampires guarding the village but they were quickly taken care of with a bow and arrow I had built for those who were good at archery.

We crept in taking out any vampires along the way. I couldn't believe my eyes at the fact that the vampires had only placed one guard in each place that was being protected apart from the prison, which had five guards. Three of them were taken out with the bow and arrow, but the other two moved too fast and three of our men were killed before we took out the vampires with a pure silver trip wire.

We released the captive prisoners and they took up a sword and shield each and joined the ranks happily. We slept in the nearby inn where we put twelve sentries up with a bow and arrow, a pure silver plate body, pure silver neck brace embedded with garlic and plate legs also made of pure silver so as to eliminate any hostile vampires with ease and to help defend in case they got too many vampires to cope with.

Three times that night the vampires attacked, but they were slaughtered with minimal casualties for us. In the morning we set off to the vampire fortress where there were millions of vampires and other evil creatures such as evil witches and werewolves and elemental demons. It was a long treacherous journey with many disasters mainly caused by the elemental demons and werewolves, but they had their weaknesses and we exploited these weaknesses and destroyed them. Finally we reached the fifth forest where we took up camp in a large clearing and put up fifteen sentries for extra security as we had more problems than just vampires, as ghosts were rumoured to appear at the latest hour of the night. Luckily they could be killed with silver, because it hurt their very essence and destroyed them but they still came in millions to feed on our life force.

The night passed with few incidents and we restarted the journey. We were walking through a forest when a fire elemental demon appeared, but as it was a fire demon, we threw water orbs at it and it was vanquished as the fifth hit it. We also encountered several vampires and other dark creatures including werewolves.

There was something that was starting to confuse most of us; there was a vast legion of vampires and other dark creatures yet we had come across only a few of them within the last few hours. We had a suspicion that they are planning something big, but we just didn't know what it was, so we had to find out.

We decided to split into two groups, one would carry on the journey and make camp near the castle and attack at daybreak and the second would sneak inside and find out what was going on. I decided to be in the second group and we neared the castle, we hadn't encountered anything yet which was making us a little nervous and cautious just in case something jumped out.

There was a pitch-black door with a small bat on it. We opened the door and saw twenty vampires chatting and eating, luckily they couldn't see us and we decided that we wouldn't kill them as someone might see the dead bodies and raise the alarm, which would blow the plan. We thought that the element of surprise would be the thing that won this war so we decided to keep it. Pretending to be vampires we got through relatively easily. In front of us were two werewolves guarding a door that had a sign that said –

"Do not disturb." It had a window in which we could see through and we saw a hundred werewolves guarding something we couldn't see. It seemed hopeless until I saw the small, dark ventilation shaft that led into the room. We climbed in and crept along.

We finally got to the room and we looked through and saw a load of machinery and we heard someone saying –

"This machine, when finished, will be able to merge this world with the other world and make them one large world. We will be able to take over the humans and, in doing so; will stop the prophecy coming true so we will be rulers of the world forever." We heard cheering and clapping which masked our descent from the ventilation shaft into an open piece of tubing that extended from the machinery.

Shortly afterwards, we got inside the machinery and messed with the wires and connected them to a bomb, which we set to explode in an hour. We then collected all the explosive material we could and packed it into the machine. Having programmed the bomb to explode if the machine was activated we got the hell out of there! We met up with the other squad at a clearing near the gates to the fortress and quickly told them what happened.

"*Well done,*" they said. "*All the lords are in there, the lords of all the dark creatures from what we saw. If it works then we will eliminate all but a few of the dark creatures in the world and they could be eliminated in a day.*" We ran as fast as we could from the fortress and, in what felt like seconds, the place went "boooom." We couldn't believe it; it worked. Suddenly there was a loud, commanding voice that said –

"*Well done human. You have done something that no one else has managed. You have defeated the dark creatures and for that you will be given powers, use them for good and defeat the enemy that will show itself in due time.*" I then walked away in wait for the enemy. Suddenly there was a massive explosion under me and I was carried into the air uninjured and more powerful than ever...

Christopher Cadman

The Unknown World

The rain was falling fast on the lonely, quiet street, turning what was left of the crisp white snow into slush. The mossy cobbles were slippery and everything had small raindrops falling from them. I slowly walked to the end of the garden, hoping that Id get to see what I saw the night before. I reached for the handle, slowly lifting the latch. Anxiety filled me. I gently tried opening the door. It was locked and I could hear the muffled voice of my neighbour talking loudly on the street beyond. How had it happened last night? I turned quickly and attempted to run back to the house.

Walking into the kitchen I whipped the cool water off my face and shoulders. I looked around, checking for someone else in the house. I was alone. Quickly I started frantically searching for a key. I had no idea what it would look like. I just assumed that it would look like an old fashioned, rusted key. I had no idea where it could be either; I just needed to find it. I searched madly, checking everywhere. I moved every item in hope of finding it. Nothing was left unturned. I opened the last cupboard in desperate hope. I moved the many cereal boxes that were there and at the back of the cupboard there was a small wooden box. It had small stars and clouds carved into it. Carefully, I lifted the latch on the box and opened the lid. There it was! The key! It was just like I imagined it. I don't know how I knew it was the key I needed, I just did.

I sprinted back down the garden, leaving the chaos in the kitchen behind. It was still raining heavily, causing me to slip on my way. I slid most of the way down the path in my mad rampage to reach the gate. I hit the gate with a bang, like heavy machinery going off. Slowly, I reached into my pocket, pulling out the cold key. It felt cool and hard against my soft wet skin, I watched quietly as it sparkled in the sunlight as I tilted it. I placed it in the lock. I felt a wave of anxiety fill me, almost consuming my mind and causing me to rush. I turned the key and got a firm grasp on the handle of the door. Now was the time. I lifted the latch and pushed the gate. It opened.

A warm, welcoming breeze hit me. All my body shuddered. I'd not felt the warmth of summer in some time. I opened my eyes. I was shocked to see a different place to last night, but still what I saw amazed me. It was like nothing I'd ever seen before. It was a new world. I carefully moved forwards into the new world. Making sure not to slip on the iced ledge before the opening. For a moment I just stood there, calmly taking in my surroundings. The warm breeze was like a gentle hand, moving my hair. I was in a large forest with tall dark trees all around me. Specks of sunlight breaking through the tree canopy occasionally broke the thick blackness. It looked like any normal woods, yet had an air of primeval mystery to it.

I grasped behind me, feeling for the handle of the garden gate. But instead I got a handful of thick thorns. The door had disappeared. Panic filled me as I frantically started pulling at the bush behind me. Why wasn't it there? Where had it gone? How would I ever get back? All these questions rushed into my head and I started to think about what my mum would be thinking. I could just imagine her face when she walked into the kitchen. But then I was thrust back to where I was by a strong cold wind. This calmed me slightly. It would be okay I thought. I had got here through a door and I could get back through a door. I could just wait.

I moved to a tree not far from where I had arrived and sat up against its large trunk. I kept my eyes constantly fixed on where the door had been. Minutes passed. Minutes turned into hours, but still no door. I started to drift off, but I didn't know this place so I forced myself to stay awake. More time passed, but still there was no door. I realised that nothing was going to happen so I changed my objective and got up. It was darker now and a light mist had set in across the ground. It felt ghostly walking through the lonely forest. My eyes were always watching for a way home. The forest was almost alive now. Constantly moving. Squirrels moved in the hollowed out trees and along branches and I was sure they were talking like I would. Badgers had left their homes, only they were bigger and I could swear one badger had a dressing gown on.

I kept walking but I still couldn't find anything. I changed directions on the path and started to walk to the right. After just a few steps I could see something ahead. It was a dark and sinister looking clearing. All the plants around it had died and withered away. It started to move closer as I stood there looking. I was too terrified to move. Something about the place had me glued to the ground under me. As it got closer I could see someone or something stood in the middle of it. It looked to be a large hooded figure. I was at the edge of the clearing by now; just close enough to feel the icy breeze coming from whatever it was in there.

"Who's there?" I shouted. My voice was trembling along with my body. No one replied. Suddenly I got my legs back and I started to walk slowly forwards. The figure didn't move though, it just stood still. Like it was waiting for me.

Moving closer to it I realised it wasn't a person it was a door; a large wooden door! Relief flooded into me like a strong wave. I ran towards it, ran as fast as I could. I didn't even stop to think about where the door could lead to, or to notice that it was a completely different door. I just pushed open the door and ran through. What a massive mistake I had made. The door shut behind me, and left me in complete darkness. There was a loud noise and suddenly.... I dropped.

Cloe Jackson

Spirit World

The cold, damp night airs wrapped around him like a blanket. The world was silent and nothing seemed to exist. Steve wandered warily through the darkness. It seemed as though the places he visited were dead. However, nothing could stop him carrying on through this mysterious land.

Suddenly there was the harsh cry of a bird. Steve turned, looking terrified, but amazingly nothing unusual was there. He slowly turned away from the screeching bird. He couldn't see far ahead but he noticed some vague lights in the distance and hoped it was a village. It was strange because everything was silent. As he crept closer the lights brightened as if they knew he was there. Now he could hear noises. Many sleeping people lay spread-eagled with their backs on the ground, all snoring heavily.

Steve edged towards the closest being. His heart beat faster as he leaned over the body. From what Steve could see it was a man. A putrid smell oozed from the man's mouth.

Steve poked him with a stick. Expecting him to wake, Steve was disappointed when he didn't. Instead the man simply grunted and rolled over. On the man's back Steve saw many slashes, some of which seemed to still be bleeding. The sight made Steve shiver with fright. He moved on through the village, looking carefully at the surroundings.

As he wandered through the village he saw piles of old bones and rotting flesh. The sight made Steve wonder where he was. What kind of people pile bones around themselves? Who would want the smell of rotting flesh following them everywhere they went in the village?

Just ahead of him Steve saw a huge ghostly statue in front of a large castle-like hut. The statue was weathered down so much that he couldn't make out any of the features. The wind was whistling through the dead trees and grasping his cold ears. Steve shivered again.

He crept around the tall, dark statue where he could finally see the hut. The hut was as large as a four-storey house. It was made purely of mud and straw. Steve noticed that, unlike the other huts, this had what could be described as a garden. However, all of the plants and grasses were dead. Inside Steve could see a huge object in the centre of the room.

As he moved closer towards the door he realised that it was a body. Flies buzzed around piles of bones and rotting flesh. The piles in the hut were much larger than the piles around the village. The stench from the hut was horrendous. Steve had to hold back the vomit that was climbing up his throat as he crept closer to the body.

A loud groan came from the direction of the body, the noise dispersed around the village. Steve jumped in terror. He hadn't expected such a noise like that. Scared that he had woken the beast Steve lowered his body until he was curled up into a ball.

After a few minutes had passed, Steve straightened up against a muddy wall. A hard ball of mud fell off of the wall and crashed into his back. He let out an almighty roar!

The body lying on the ground suddenly leapt up and ran towards Steve. Knowing what he had done Steve sprinted towards the exit. The beast ran straight into the wall and fell like a tonne of bricks to the ground, unconscious.

Steve ran into the night towards the forest, when suddenly a hole appeared out of nowhere. He managed to avoid the tragedy of falling into the hole and then he started to run towards the forest. Shortly afterwards, a large, red abysmal demon jumped out of the hole. Its glowing eyes glazed towards him, its horns gaped out of its skull, its black chest heaved as it breathed heavily, hot steam shot out of its nostrils and evaporated into the air. As Steve tried to escape, its long, red, muscled arms started clawing at Steve. Its long nails nearly reached him and narrowly missed slashing open his throat.

Steve, with a sudden burst of energy, leapt away from the demon. The night air filled with screams of anger. The roaring echoed through the village and into the forest. Its eyes were crimson with rage and its arms flapped wildly as it tried to move forwards, but it slipped and fell backwards into the abyss.

Steve turned again to run towards the forest and escape when he felt himself lifting up off of the ground. He kept rising and rising until he was above the trees, but still he kept rising. He was as light as a feather. He spiralled in the air and kept spiralling until...

Steve woke up in hot sweats, he was panting like a wild animal. He nervously looked around the room to make sure that there was nothing there. Realising there wasn't and that he had been dreaming he lay back on his bed thinking about what he had just seen.

Was it a dream? Had it really happened? Did the village really exist? Steve would never know...

Benjamin Sidebottom and Corey Warrior

SECTOR XIII

Introduction
New York City
Earth
Sprawling masses of concrete, glass buildings and pavements stretched for miles. Cars and lorries hurtled down the roads and people wandered the streets going about their business amid the hustle of daily life. On top of the highest building stood a lone figure dressed in black and carrying an impossibly long sword, his grey hair obscuring his face. He surveyed his surroundings –

"A fine kingdom… soon it will all be mine."

Chapter 1
Dragonmoon fortress
Dramnor

*"Where is he…Tell me where has he gone? ………
Speak."* Edward Dragonmoon slapped a metal gauntlet across the face of the captured warrior, but still he said nothing. *"Take this scum to the dungeons maybe then he will talk,"* he motioned to a guard who took the prisoner away. Edward left the room heading down the corridor. His greaves and boots clanked as he paced towards the great hall, where he knew the council were sat eagerly awaiting him. He paused and adjusting his armour, he pushed open the great oak doors into the great hall of Dragonmoon. Around the room sat over two hundred men, dwarves, elves, satyrs, centaurs, dragoons and Wyrmkin. Steeling himself, he strode to the far side of the room to the throne. Silence fell over the room like a thick blanket.

"Greetings, there is no easy way to put this, but somehow the fiend Fang Flameheart has gone missing." The whole room was in uproar, with creatures everywhere shouting in enraged fear. It shocked everyone there who knew the legend of Fang, a demon lord that had broken his bonds from hell and had nearly succeeded in taking control over all the lands of Dramnor. It had taken Edward's father the former king of Dragonmoon everything he had to defeat him, but in doing so he had to put his soul in his sword which killed him.

Until now everything had been fine for Dramnor, but some of Fang's warriors had killed the guards that held him prisoner in the nether vortex. Now he was free to do as he wished, but no one could find him. It was as if he had vanished into thin air.

"And what do ye propose we do about this problem?" Morgirim Bronzefeather asked. Morgirim was the king of the dwarves and he had a reputation for being a stalwart warrior slaying hundreds with the legendary rune hammer of the dwarven lords.

"I am afraid that there is nothing we can do."

"I beg to differ," a cold voice commented from out of the shadows. The cloaked figure stepped forward with a long stave clutched in his grip. Long grey hair fell across his face, *"We could use sector XIII."*

"No I have told you many times that we can't do that."

"What be this sector XIII?" Kal asked. Kal was a Wyrmkin Bull.

"Sector XIII is an elite group of guardians. They are powerful and ageless but my father's dying words were 'don't trust sector XIII' and to this day I haven't."

"Well that's no reason not to trust us," the cloaked figure's voice rang out.

"The council of elders will decide as has always been the way. Step forward representatives of the seven point star." The crowds of creatures moved forward in anticipation and a human in full mail armour carrying a golden spear stepped into the centre of the room. He was called Medive and was followed by Morgirim and then an elf called Furion, who was dressed in braided leather armour and held two knives. He was followed by a satyr named Kar, who held a mace. Next a four-armed dragoon known as Drakarth held two pairs of duelling sabres and finally Kal held a scythe.

Edward stepped down from the throne carrying the split sword of Dragonmoon.

"All those in favour of sector XIII raise your hand now." Four of the seven raised their hands and moved to the right side of Edward and the three against moved to the left side of Edward and sighed.

"So it has come to pass that sector XIII will come to power, council adjourned." Edward looked around to see the reaction of the cloaked man but he was gone.

Chapter 2
The cellar of the Scarlet Raven inn
Dramnor

Black candles burned around the room casting an unnatural light on the faces of the occupants. Thirteen figures stood around the room each holding their weapons.

"The time has come my friends. Sector XIII has finally come to power in the eyes of that tyrant

Dragonmoon. Operations will continue as planned No's II, III, IV, V, VI and VII will go to northern Dramnor and pretend to search for Fang while No's VIII, IX, X, XI, X1I, XIII will activate the portal. I have some business at the nether vortex. By the time I'm done everything will be complete! Within two days Dramnor will be ours and earth is ours for the taking!"

Dragonmoon fortress
Dramnor

"How could this happen? I thought that you said we had the support of the whole council? Sector XIII should never have come to power!"

"My lord I did my best but only the dwarves, elves and humans would listen to us. The others have broken the alliance."

"Then they shall be cast from my hall," Edward Dragonmoon raged. *"The alliance was formed to keep Fang away from our cities and towns and now he is free. If I don't have their full support, I fear that the council will be disbanded."*

"So be it your lordship." The elf walked out of the room leaving Edward to his thoughts. As soon as the elf was out of the room, he peeled the mask from his face. Casting it in the fire, he pulled his black cloak from his backpack pressing his fingertips to his scarred temples as he sent out his thoughts.

"Number II finished," he reported and with that he disappeared.

Dragonmoon dungeons

An old man with a bushy beard walked into the dungeons, a thick leather pouch at his hip. The guards stopped him, before he had even taken two steps into the room.

"And where do we think we're going now? There are no unauthorized visits." The man said nothing, but raised one hand now alight with fire and launched a beam of it into the nearest guard. He swung the beam around the room incinerating all the guards and extinguished the flame with a flick of his hand. Then he stopped and began channelling dark energy into the room. Out of the energy from his hands came five demons. With a flick of his wrists he sent them into the prison cells. Within two minutes they were all back with the dead bodies of ten prisoners. He set to work with a knife cutting a hole into the heart of each. Once the heart was exposed, he reached into his pouch pulled ten crystals from it and placed a crystal on each heart. Then channelling more energy, he drained the souls from the prisoners. When this was done he placed his fingertips on his temples and reached out his thoughts –

"Number III finished." Wrapping the black cloak around him he disappeared.

Dragonmoon gunpowder store

The gunpowder store was calm, with the guards sat around drinking ale with the dwarven king. Just as a guard passed him another pot of ale, the doors exploded and as six spears span around, a black cloaked warrior, stood in the door. The king was drunk at this point so he stood up calmly.

"Ah my friend from sector XIII what brings you here at this time of night?" The figure did not answer. He merely lashed a spear at the king's head knocking him out and before the others had time to react; the figure

had slashed out at the others killing them. He then pulled from his pocket a small pouch, he flung it into the gunpowder and it exploded. His thoughts reached out like the others –

"Number IV finished."

Dragonmoon throne room

"Why is this all happening? I've got reports coming in of cloaked assassins, spear wielding warriors and demons. The gunpowder store has been destroyed, the dungeons have been emptied, every prisoner is dead and their souls have been taken. The alliance has fallen and my kingdom is in shambles."

"All is not lost my lord, you are still king of Dragonmoon, are you not?" asked his advisor Stephan. He ran a hand through his beard, *"You may not rule over a lot anymore, but a king you still remain."*

"A king that has no power anymore," he shouted.

"If you are going to be like this, I am afraid that I can't help you." With that he walked out of the room and walked down the corridor into a room. His face melted revealing his face to be burned horrifically. He pulled a metal circle from his pocket. Staring into it he studied his reflection. He then looked closer and saw a man in a black cloak.

"Number I" he said.

"Here," he replied. *"Is it done?"* number I asked.

"Yes," he said. The cloaked man laughed.

"Good then, get to Infernus and tell Sharpshooter to pay Dragonmoon a visit." The man wiped the disk and then looked again.

"Sharpshooter?"

"Here," a gravelly voice answered.

OUT OF THE SHADOWS

"Number 1 says that you need to pay Dragonmoon fortress a visit." Sharpshooter didn't answer for a while.

"Metal manipulator leave my blade bullets out front, I'll be there in five." He placed the disk back in his robes and pulled out two bullet magazines. He then threw them out of the window and into the front courtyard. A man appeared instantly dressed in a black robe. He caught them and slipped them into his pockets. He pulled out from his belt two gun blades that looked like oversized revolvers with blades at the end of the barrels. Pulling the magazines from his pockets he slipped them into the guns. Taking aim he looked at the highest tower of Dragonmoon and fired blowing off the roof of the tower. Soldiers swarmed out of the fortress in response to this.

"Humph a little competition..." he readjusted his sights and fired rapidly, bullets raining through the soldiers and leaving gaping wounds. As he ran out of bullets he used the blades to slash at the soldiers, cutting down many of them with vicious slashes leaving the ground sodden with blood. Running into a clearing he shouted –

"Reload" and his guns reloaded. He fired off a series of shots into the fortress shattering stones all over the fortress. A few more bullets and the whole battalion of soldiers were defeated. Reloading again he fired at the fortress shattering one whole wall only. When he saw Edward Dragonmoon come to the window he called –

"Sector XIII sends their regards."

The twisting nether
Dramnor

The twisting nether wasn't the sort of place you wanted to visit and it certainly wasn't the sort of place you

191

wanted to be made a prisoner in, but that was the fate of the warlord Hydraxxx, sentenced to life imprisonment in the nether for trying to control Dramnor. Now he was stuck in the heart of the nether surrounded by werepyre guards. These guards were always on the look-out, but they did not notice the man in black until it was too late. His staff cracked one on the head and he fell into the jaws of a nether stalker. The man raced around attacking guards with his staff. He killed two, but then suddenly the guards stopped trying to kill him and they transformed into full werepyres, with huge fangs, claws and wings.

"Our turn now little man," one managed to say before his teeth grew. The man stopped and pulled his stave apart revealing a ridiculously long sword. He threw off his cloak and his grey hair flowed. The light from the nether shone off his steel shoulder guards and the metal rivets that covered the clothes he wore.

"You were saying Fido?" With a grin he launched himself at the one that had spoken and decapitated him as he flew past. The effect on the others was instant. They all lashed out at the man. He blocked their strikes with speed and counter-attacked slaying them all. He chuckled -

"Too easy!" He reached into his pocket and pulled a golden necklace from it. It had a strange stone at its centre. He slipped it on and stared into the heart of the nether. Channelling the energy of the nether he brought Hydraxxx to the surface.

"Freedom at last..........but who are you?" he bellowed.

"Number I, let's just say I am a friend. I have a proposition for you..."

"And what would that be?"

"My friends and I have a bit of bad blood, with the Dragonmoons. I understand that this is also the case with you."

"Yes that's true. What is this bargain of yours?"

"I want you to keep Dragonmoon and his forces at bay while sector XIII leaves Dramnor, via the portal atop mount Infernus."

"And what do I get?"

"Control of Dramnor and the creatures of the nether at your command." This was a bargain that Hydraxxx couldn't refuse.

"Done," he rasped. With that number I pointed his sword into the heart of the nether and the nether shattered releasing hordes of creatures some huge like the swarm of dragons and some small like the demon mice that scurried by. Hydraxxx was the last to leave, brandishing his fabled war blade.

"Onward my warriors to Dragonmoon fortress," he roared. Number I smiled. His sword bloodied, he flew across the whole of Dramnor over the seas of time and the golden forests of Hyjar, towards the peak of mount Infernus where he saw the rest of sector XIII waiting for him. As he landed and took his place in the circle he saw the faces of the others. The scarred face of the 'sharp shooter,' the bearded 'soul stealer,' the shadow masked 'whirlwind lancer,' and 'the gambler of fate' shuffling his cards, the knives of the long haired 'assassin' gleaming, the right and left blade mirror images of each other, the burned face of 'the metal manipulator', the mute 'silent hero,' the tattooed 'behemoth,' the smart talking 'devious schemer' and 'destiny,' all with weapons at the ready.

"So finally the hour has come to pass my friends. As we speak Hydraxxx and his army are marching on towards Dragonmoon fortress. The portal will soon be ready and we will conquer the world that waits." He paused, *"I trust that you have got the soul stones,"* he asked the soul stealer. He nodded and revealed his hip pouch. It was filled with stones that glowed a deep red. *"Good then there is only one thing that we need to do before we leave, the spirit of Edward Dragonmoon must be snuffed out."*

"You're not going to get the chance traitor," screamed a voice and then leaping over a nearby ridge was Edward Dragonmoon, brandishing the split sword.

"How amusing this makes the job more easy; Sharpshooter, activate the meta pod." Sharpshooter reached into a pocket and pulled out a metal disk with a raised button. He pressed the button and the castle in the distance was instantly engulfed in a bright white light.

"Noooooo.........my kingdom."

"Never mind now my brother, it will be over soon."

"Brother - what are you talking about?"

"Oh didn't dad tell you? It wasn't Fang Flameheart that he killed himself to defeat ....it was Fang Dragonmoon." With that Edward launched himself at his brother who parried the blow easily.

"Tut, tut, tut. you didn't do a good job with my kingdom did you, but then again you were more interested in your stupid alliance, too blinded by it that you didn't realise that all your power was almost stolen out from under you. Your adviser was the metal manipulator in disguise, the ambassador was the sharp shooter in a mask. The real ambassador was killed, before he even set

foot into your city, we have always been here, where you least expect us."

"Shut up, shut up just shut up," Edward cried as he launched himself once again, this time scratching Fang's shoulder guard. Fang just laughed.

"Is that the best that you've got?" Suddenly without warning, Fang lashed out impaling his brother with his sword right down to the handle. *"Sorry brother but nothing personal."* He pulled the sword free wiping it clean on the cloak of Edward.

"Well that takes care of all our problems activate the portal." The soul stealer threw the soul stones in the air. They floated in a circle, lightning flowing between them. A light shone through the portal and through it they could see a different world, a barren desert.

"A new life and a new world to conquer," said the lancer and he walked through the portal first. Everyone else followed suit, except Fang, he stopped a moment by his brother's corpse. He laid the split sword along his chest and placed his brother's hands on the handle.

"You always wanted to be like our father. Now lay in peace like him." With that he walked back through the portal.

Chapter 3
The Sahara desert
Africa
The desert was scorching hot and it seemed to stretch endlessly.

"Not much of a new world," said Behemoth.

"This is the wrong place. We need to get to New York City. This is Africa," said Fang.

195

"And how exactly do you know that?" asked the destiny warrior. He seemed at unrest and was fiddling with something in his pocket.

"*The internet,*" he replied. "*In the short time I was here I found a lot out.*" All the warriors rose silently and began flying towards America.

"*How exactly are we going to take over this city you speak of?*"

"Simple," but he wouldn't say any more. As they arrived a large sign proclaimed that they were at anchorage Alaska. The bleak landscape and snow made for an uninviting landscape.

"*Well where's the city?*" snapped Destiny.

"*If you'd waited a minute I could have told you that we have gone too far north, but this is perfect. We can bring the army through.*"

"Army?" asked Whirlwind lancer.

"*Yes army,*" Sharpshooter answered. "*What did you think the meta pod actually did.........destroyed the city ....You are too narrow minded. We transformed the city dwellers and Hydraxxx and his army to Shadekin.*"

"*And now we plan to bring them back through,*" said Fang. With that said, the soul stealer threw the soul stones into the air. They spun into a ring which crackled with energy and through the circle of stones the city of Dragonmoon could be seen. Fang walked over calmly, discarding his cloak as he did so, he reached the portal and stopped. He shouted through –

"*Hydraxxx get yourself here and bring the rest.*" A bellow came from the portal and Hydraxxx stepped through, but he was ethereal, almost like he was on the verge of crossing over to the next world. He seemed unsteady on his feet.

"*I live to serve lord,*" he rasped.

"*Good,*" Fang answered. "*When I was here last, I heard of a structure that could be of use to us, I believe that the humans call it the World Trade Centre.*"

"*And how could this be of use to us?*" asked the left and right blade simultaneously.

"*It is a tall structure and it offers protection because if anyone tries to follow us, they have to fight their way through our entire army …A perfect citadel for our empire,*" said Soul Stealer.

"*Well what are we waiting for?*" yelled Behemoth.

They all flew up into the air and towards the World Trade Centre, with Hydraxxx and an army of humans, dwarves, elves, satyrs, dragons and Wyrmkin. Amongst them were the warriors of the star, still dressed in their armour. As the army reached the border of Alaska Fang stopped.

"*What is it?*" asked Lancer. "*This is going to take too long. We're going to port in.*" With that said he drew his sword and drew a circle in the air. The circle glowed with energy as it grew to five metres across; everyone stepped through and in an instant the scene changed from the bleak snow of Alaska to the sprawling metropolis of New York City. In front of them lay the World Trade Centre.

Sector XIII went straight to the top of the towers. While the army surrounded the towers the warriors of the star also floated halfway up the tower. Their arrival had caused chaos in the streets with people racing away from the army of creatures released from the nether, and the Shadekin who were killing all who were within reach. Through all the confusion two planes could be seen hurtling towards the towers, Fang saw this also and lashed out sending a shockwave towards them. This knocked them off course. They crashed in the streets.

"*Hear me now people of earth we are your new masters and nothing will stop us,*" Fang cried. With that the metal manipulator pulled another meta pod from his robe. This one was red though he passed this to Fang.

"*Now you will see a small fraction of our power.*" With that he pressed it and all electricity in the world was drawn into the pod plunging the world into chaos.

Chapter 4
10,000 years later
Earth

The sprawling masses of concrete towers that once dominated the New York skyline were gone. The only thing that remained was the World Trade Centre and that was a shadow of what it once was. A twisted mould had crept up its walls turning them a deep blood red and atop the tower sat the thirteen lords of the world. Sector XIII had grown in power during their ten thousand year reign so much so, that the whole world was under their control and due to the meta pod that activated on the eleventh of September the whole world had been reduced to a shamanistic culture of warriors. Many people were left totally helpless because of their lack of electricity and the world shattered into a wandering culture of tribes. This made it easier for the sector to control them and that was how the world stayed for the next ten thousand years. Sector XIII controlled everything and everyone. Many humans were changed into Shadekin forced into service by the sector and day by day, year by year their power grew until they grew too powerful and attracted the attention of the creature known as the devourer. This was a hideous creature whose only intention was to bring pain and suffering.

New York
Earth
The once bustling streets were quiet; the once congested roads empty. The only things that moved were the Shadekin and the armies of the XIII. Fang had chosen New York for his personal seat of power. It reminded him of Dramnor.

That particular day was like any other. It got to around 12 o'clock and an ear splitting wail cried out from the skies. Within seconds the whole of sector XIII had teleported to the Empire State building, which was now a broken ruin of what it once was. Scanning the skies they saw nothing until a hand swooped down through the clouds clearing them and they realised what it was. The devourer was here. The whole of Sector XIII knew of his legacy and his powers and feared him.

"*What do you want foul beast?*" Fang called to him.

"*You have something I want feeble shade,*" he screeched back. His voice was like nails being drawn over a chalkboard.

"*And what would that be?*" XIII asked.

"*Power!*" The one word was screeched back.

"*Well if that's what you wanted you only had to ask,*" replied V calmly. Sector XIII gathered into a circle focusing their strength into a pool of energy that glowed. Crackled lightning flashed and smouldered everything around them. Suddenly the energy ball flew upwards into the writhing face of the devourer. The beast fell back stunned. The power fired at him was too much for him to bear so he flew away cursing the sector and all of its members. The people of earth saw it flying away and realised that it would take an extreme power indeed to get rid of the sector.

Chapter 5
Half-moon forest just outside New York
America
Earth
The bonfire blazed in the middle of the clearing. Men sat around it, the flames throwing dancing shadows across their faces. One fidgety youth sat away from the group, whittling a stick to a point. A tall man stood up. He appeared to be the leader of the group.

"This year's crop appears to be better than last time." The fidgety youth stood up at this, throwing his spear aside.

"So what if the crop was good? If we don't get half the food it doesn't matter."

"Kai sit down. You were not asked to speak." The youth took off into the forest, his knife hanging at his side. He ran and ran until he arrived at an old missile silo. He hid in the forest. He had found it 5 years ago and had been coming here ever since. The youth prised open the old doors that creaked through lack of being oiled. He peered down into the gloom. The familiar staircase creaked as the wind whistled through the cracks in the doors. He stepped down tentatively onto the first step that creaked under his weight. He carried on down the stairs feeling his way along the wall. The familiar cracks and bumps created a mental picture of the layout of the

tunnel. Once at the bottom he heard his feet hit metal. The sound resonated around the room. He carried on towards the centre of the silo.

A stone altar stood in the centre of the chamber. Kai reached out, the stone crumbling under his fingers. His fingers curled around the hilt of the sword that lay there; the metal feeling cold in his grasp. The sword had belonged to Kai's great, great, great grandfather who had been one of the shaman, a renegade group of sorcerers who had harnessed the power of spirits, channelling their energies into weapons. They had been the last hope of the people of earth, but like every thing and everyone that had stood in the way of the sector, they had been swept aside.

"*Grandfather, give me a sign that things will be better please,*" Kai whispered into the dark. After a while nothing had happened and angrily Kai cast the sword aside. It danced away the blade glinting in the dark. Kai realised what he had done and raced to the sword.

He stopped, realising that something was wrong. He couldn't think what it was until the sword began glowing red. A sense of dread swept through Kai. His father had told him stories of when his grandfather was a shaman. He recalled one tale where his father had described *"spirit unity,"* which was when the shaman would power his weapon with a spirit. This was just as his father had described, tentatively he reached out to touch the blade. It sparked at him three times before he could grasp it, once he held it the glow turned brighter until it hurt his eyes to look at it. He felt another presence in the chamber, his heart was beating wildly and for the first time in his life he felt afraid.

Kai opened his eyes slowly. The glow had dimmed and in front of him stood a ghostly warrior in full armour carrying a sword that was exactly the same as the one held in Kai's grasp, with the razor sharp cutting edge and the wing shaped hand guard.

"*Who are you?*" whispered Kai.

"*I am Cervantes and you must be Kai. I've been waiting for you.*"

"*Waiting for me, why?!*"

"*Yes, your great grandfather said that one of his descendants would come back here and release me and now you have.*"

"*How did I release you?*" Kai wondered to himself. As if he had read his thoughts the ghost pointed to where Kai had thrown his sword. A red crystal lay shattered.

"*Firstly, I can read your thoughts. Secondly my soul was kept in that crystal. When you threw the sword, you broke the seal that kept me locked in.*" Kai's head was spinning. It was all too much to bear. He broke and ran, the sword swinging at his side. As he ran he felt a strange energy run through him and his hand felt warm. Looking down a metal glove was forming around his hand and began creeping up his arm. He stopped trying to claw it from his arm. The warm feeling spread throughout his body and so did the metal, until he was covered in armour like the ghost of Cervantes, except the helmet, which didn't form. The sword was now stuck to his hand and it began to glow red another time. The ghost of Cervantes appeared once again –

"*You cannot run from your destiny Kai.*"

Scott Boardman

Printed in the United Kingdom
by Lightning Source UK Ltd.
133376UK00001B/16-42/P